The Armourer's House

ROSEMARY SUTCLIFF

The Armourer's House

Illustrated by
C. WALTER HODGES

London
OXFORD UNIVERSITY PRESS
1973

Oxford University Press, Ely House, London W. 1

GLASGOW NEW YORK TORONTO MELBOURNE WELLINGTON
CAPE TOWN IBADAN NAIROBI DAR ES SALAAM LUSAKA ADDIS ABABA
DELHI BOMBAY CALCUTTA MADRAS KARACHI LAHORE DACCA
KUALA LUMPUR SINGAPORE HONG KONG TOKYO

ISBN 0 19 272037 6

First published 1951
Second impression 1957
First published in the Oxford Children's Library series 1962
First published in this edition 1973

All rights reserved. No part of this publication may be reproduced, stored in a re-
trieval system, or transmitted, in any form or by any means, electronic, mechanical,
photocopying, recording or otherwise, without the prior permission of Oxford University
Press

This book is sold subject to the condition that it shall not, by way of trade or otherwise,
be lent, re-sold, hired out, or otherwise circulated without the publisher's prior consent
in any form of binding or cover other than that in which it is published and without a
similar condition including this condition being imposed on the subsequent purchaser.

Printed in Holland
Zuid-Nederlandsche Drukkerij N.V.
's-Hertogenbosch

CONTENTS

1 *Sails at Billingsgate*

Tamsyn Caunter stood on the doorstep of the little grey house and watched the grey sky above the tree-tops, and shivered in the grey March wind that seemed somehow colder than any wind she had ever known before. Her Uncle Martin, who had come out from Bideford to see her off on her journey, stood on the doorstep too, holding her hand in a large, warm, consoling clasp, and talking cheerfully about the glories of London Town; but he was almost as miserable as she was, and they were both listening all the time for the clip-clop of horses' hooves on the cobbles, because Uncle Gideon had just gone to bring round the horse on which he was going to carry Tamsyn away to London.

The little grey house had been Tamsyn's home ever since she could remember, because she had been such a very small baby when her parents died and she came to live there with Grandmother, that there might just as well not have been a beforetime at all, as far as she was concerned. And now Grandmother was dead, too, and Tamsyn must go right away and live with Uncle Gideon, whom she had never seen until three days ago, and with his family, whom she had never seen at all; she must leave behind her all the things and people she loved, like Uncle Martin and Sibbly the Cook. That was

1

why she was so desperately unhappy; not because of Grandmother, for she had never really been very close to Grandmother, who was the sort of person you respect enormously but do not dare to love.

'If only I could have gone to live with Uncle Martin!' she thought desperately.

Uncle Martin was a merchant of Bideford Town (what people call a 'Merchant Venturer'), and had two ships of his own trading with countries half the world away, and a third ship a-building in Master Braund's shipyard, that was to be swifter and more beautiful than either of them. She was to be called the *Joyous Venture* because she was to join in the new trade with the West Indies, which would be a very great adventure indeed. It would have been lovely to have gone and lived with Uncle Martin, and watched the *Joyous Venture* built, and seen the tall ships come and go; but he was not married, and Grandmother had not thought that anyone could bring up a little girl really properly without a wife to help him; so she had arranged long ago that Tamsyn was to go and live with Uncle Gideon, because *he* had Aunt Deborah.

But Tamsyn did not want to be brought up properly, she only wanted to be happy, and she gave a small, woeful sniff.

'Think how nice it will be to have other children to play with!' said Uncle Martin heartily, as though in answer to the sniff. But Tamsyn did not want other children, she much preferred ships. 'And of course you could always come home when you are grown up,' said Uncle Martin, even more heartily.

That did cheer her a little, though being grown up seemed a long way off, because she was not quite nine yet; and she stifled the next sniff.

And next moment she heard the clatter of hooves she had been listening for, and Uncle Gideon came riding round the corner of the house and reined in before the door, looking down at the two of them in a grave, kindly sort of way. 'I think it would be as well if we started at once,' said Uncle Gideon.

Tamsyn's few belongings had already been stowed in the saddle-bags, and she had said good-bye to fat, kind Sibbly the Cook, who was now crying in the back kitchen with her apron over her head; and there was nothing to wait for. So she and Uncle Martin hugged each other good-bye, while Uncle Gideon sat his fidgeting horse and watched a rook flapping up into the wind, as though he had never seen one before.

'Why aren't you a boy, Tamsy?' Uncle Martin demanded indignantly at the last moment. 'Then Grandmother would never have got this crotchet into her head, and you could have come and lived with me, and later on you should have been Master of the *Joyous Venture*.'

2

'I wish I was a boy,' gulped Tamsyn. 'Oh, I *wish* I was!' She had always wished that ever since she could remember, so that one day she could have sailed out over the Bar with one of those tall ships of Bideford Town and seen all the strange and wonderful things that sailors talked about when they came home again from their voyages. But she had never wished it half as much as she did now.

But it was no good wishing; and it was time to go. Tamsyn managed not to cling to Uncle Martin when he stopped hugging her and lifted her up to the pillion saddle; she twisted her hands obediently in Uncle Gideon's belt, when he told her to; and when he asked her if she was All Right Behind, she said she was, in a voice that hardly wobbled at all.

So Uncle Gideon leaned down and gripped hands with Uncle Martin, and said, 'See you in London one of these days, Martin.'

And Uncle Martin said very cheerfully, 'Aye, that you will, old lad, I shall come up to see my Tamsy before any of us are much older.'

Then Uncle Gideon touched his heel to the horse's flank, and they were off and away, tittupping over the moss-grown cobbles. Tamsyn looked round once, as they swung out through the gateway into the steep lane that led down to Bideford; and the last she saw of Uncle Martin, he was standing where they had left him, waving after them, with his flat merchant's cap slipping wildly over one ear. (Uncle Martin never could keep his cap on straight, because his red hair stood so very much on end.) 'Good-bye,' he called. 'Good-bye, my honey!'

Tamsyn waved back, but she could not call in answer, because there was a large aching lump in her throat, and by the time she had swallowed it, the tall, wind-swayed hedge was between them, and she could not see Uncle Martin any more.

Tamsyn rode all across England, sitting on the pillion behind Uncle Gideon and holding tight to his belt so as not to fall off; and it took them a whole week to do the journey. Every night they stopped at an inn, and Tamsyn was handed over to the innkeeper's wife, and sometimes the innkeeper's wife was nice, and sometimes she was not. Every morning she was lifted up again behind Uncle Gideon and they set out on the long day's ride, just like yesterday and the day before. Uncle Gideon was very kind to her in a quiet sort of way, but it seemed a dreary week all the same, and the March winds blew very cold, and Tamsyn was very homesick and desperately low in her inside; and by the time they rode through the village of Charing and up the road between great houses and broad gardens that was called the Strand, and clattered through Ludgate into London Town, she was so stiff and cold and tired and unhappy that she hardly knew where she was.

There seemed to Tamsyn to be a terrifying number of people in Uncle Gideon's house!

First there was Uncle Gideon himself, who was a Master Swordsmith and Armourer. He was long and lean and quiet and kindly, with grey hairs in his red beard. (All the Caunters had red hair except Tamsyn, whose hair was black instead.) He had a rather sad face, and a queer way of talking, so that you were never quite sure if he was laughing at you; and he looked really much more like a scholar than a swordsmith.

Then there was Aunt Deborah, who was warm and pretty, and had honey-coloured hair, which she coiled up under a black velvet hood like the ones the queens wear on playing-cards, because most ladies wore it like that in those days. Her eyes were blue as speedwell and when they went all starry, so that she looked like someone in a stained-glass window with the sun shining through it, she was generally wondering what she should give Uncle Gideon for supper, or whether she had enough fine holland over from making a shift for Beatrix to make a shirt for Littlest.

Then there were the children.

Piers was the eldest. He was fourteen and a bit, and apprenticed to his father, so that one day he would be a swordsmith too. He was quite distressingly ugly, with rufty-tufty dark red hair, and very large ears, and a bony sort of face with a beaky sort of nose covered in freckles. But somehow, when he started doing anything with his hands, such as mending a broken toy or rubbing Bunch, the little Italian greyhound, behind the ears, you forgot about his being ugly. He was a peaceable and quiet sort of person, and he had a way of going off by himself sometimes, and the Almost-Twins said he was dull, though they found him very useful when they wanted anything mended or a drawing made—because the things that Piers drew always looked alive. But from the very first moment that she saw him, Tamsyn did not think that Piers was dull. She thought he was probably a most exciting person, only the exciting part was underneath, so that it didn't show.

The Almost-Twins came next. There was Beatrix who was rising eleven and had a delicate nose and hair as red as flame, and hated getting dirty or sticky or her feet wet, just like a cat. And there was Giles, who was practically ten. He had a delicate nose and hair as red as flame, too (though he did not mind at all about getting dirty or sticky *or* his feet wet), so that people often thought they were twins. Beatrix was generally pretending to be somebody else; most often it was Catherine of Aragon, but sometimes it was other people, so that nobody ever knew, when she came down in the mornings, whether she was Queen Catherine in Prison, or Mistress Whitcome-two-doors-down-the-street, or somebody out of the Bible. Her family had got quite used to it now, so that they hardly noticed. Giles liked eating and fighting and keeping beetles and caterpillars in boxes. There had been a dreadful time when he was quite small, when he had brought a large box of snails into the house and they had escaped in the night and got simply *everywhere;* but people did not remind him of it. Not if they were wise. He and Beatrix never did anything apart if they could do it together, but they quarrelled a good deal.

Lastly there was Littlest, whose real name was Benjamin; and Littlest was round and sweet as an apple, with red cheeks and cornflower-blue eyes and straight red-gold hair. Littlest was always busy and never cross, and he was three-and-a-bit years old.

There should have been Christopher, too, the oldest of them all, and named after Tamsyn's father (though they called him Kit for short). But Kit had gone to sea and not come back, just as Tamsyn's father had done. It had all happened just after he left school, when Master Roger Whitcome, who was a silk merchant and Uncle Gideon's friend, had offered him a voyage with his ship, the *Elizabeth,* which was trading with Alexandria. Kit had wanted desperately to have just one voyage before he settled down to learning his father's trade; so he had gone. And the *Elizabeth* had gone down off the coast of Portugal in a great storm. A homeward-bound ship had saved many of the crew and brought them back to England, but not Kit. That had been nearly two years ago, and nobody seemed sad about it now; in fact they were a very gay family. But they all missed Kit, just the same, and Aunt Deborah watched the street sometimes, as though she expected to see him come walking home.

That was the family, and they were all as kind as kind could be to Tamsyn—even Beatrix when she could spare the time from being someone else—and so was Meg the Kitchen, who was inclined to be stout and inclined to be deaf and sometimes inclined to be cross, and so was Bunch. But there *were* so many of them, and there was only one of Tamsyn, and they were not her own family and she couldn't feel a bit as though they were. Anyway, she wasn't used to living with a family at all, and there were a lot of things about it that she hated. She particularly hated having to sleep in the same bed with Beatrix at night; it wasn't that Beatrix kicked or anything like that, it was just the not having a corner of her own where she could be private by herself. Beatrix didn't seem ever to want to be private; she liked an audience, all the time, so she did did not mind sharing her bed with Tamsyn; and nobody had the least idea how often Tamsyn would have cried herself to sleep, but for the fact that Beatrix would have known about it.

The house where they all lived was in a narrow street so close to the river that they could smell the mud when the tide was out, and so close to the Black Friars' Monastery that they could hear the chapel bell ringing to prayers all through the day. Every house in the street was a merchant's or a goldsmith's or something like that, but Uncle Gideon's house was the only one that belonged to an armourer; and it had a gilded helmet over the door, so that people could see at a glance that it did. It was a very narrow house, but so tall that its steep gables thrust up head and shoulders above the houses on either side, and every storey jutted out a little farther than the one below, until the topmost storey almost overhung the roof of the house over the way. It was quite a young house, and its beautiful timbering was still golden—not grey, like the weathered timbering of the really old houses in the street; and the four corbels that supported the sticking-out part of the first storey were carved into the shape of dolphins; joyous, leaping dolphins, painted bright blue. People loved brilliant colours when Henry VIII was young and gay; they dyed their stuffs and silks in all the colours of the rainbow, and wore golden sleeves and shoes of crimson velvet, and enriched their houses and their ships to match. Lots of the houses in the street had carved and painted timbers to make them beautiful. The house of Master Bodkin, the goldsmith over the way, had a lovely pattern of vines on its doorposts, and Master Roger Whitcome's doorway had its lintel carved into garlands of roses and pomegranates, all painted as gay as gay could be. But the Caunter children all liked the dolphins best, and they called the house 'the Dolphin House' because of them.

Inside the house was nice, too. The ground floor was mostly workshop, except for the kitchen and things like that, at the back. The workshop was rather dark, but when the forge fire was blown up the red light flooded into every corner in the most exciting way. It was very full of leather-topped tables and work-benches covered with tools, and the great anvil stood in a clear space in the middle, and there were little anvils too, for all the small and delicate work of the armourer's craft. And hanging on the walls and propped up on the benches were all the wonderful things that Uncle Gideon and his journeymen and prentices made for the great lords to wear and carry when they went to war or jousted with each other in the new Tilt-Yard the King's Grace had built beside Whitehall Palace; helmets of blue steel inlaid with silver, wonderfully jointed gauntlets, bright, deadly sword-blades, whole suits of armour standing in dark corners and looking terrifyingly as though there was someone inside them. It was a very busy place, the workshop, with old Caleb, the swordsmith, and the others in their leather aprons, moulding, polishing, cutting the sheets of metal with great shears; and Piers and the other prentice, whose name was Timothy, scurrying about and fetching and carrying and learning the trade; and Uncle Gideon in his long black gown overseeing the work or putting the delicate finishing touches to a piece of armour.

Timothy had one blue eye and one brown one, and he always squinted in the most enchanting way at Tamsyn and Beatrix when they came through the workshop with Aunt Deborah. (For the front door opened into the workshop, and the stairs led down into it, so that you had to go through it on your way out and in.) But Piers never did more than look up from his work for a moment. He seemed always to be so very busy learning to be an armourer.

At the top of the first flight of stairs was the guest-room, which was very beautiful, with a big bed in it hung with crimson curtains worked all over with pansies and sops-in-wine; and the parlour, where the family lived and ate and spent their evenings. The parlour was beautiful too, with panelled walls and an oriel window that had real glass in it, and a smoke-hood above the hearth carved with pomegranates for Catherine of Aragon, a pot of frilly double daffodils on the window-sill, and a chest carved with snarling leopard-heads in which Uncle Gideon kept his books. He only had three—but nobody had many in those days—one was called the Odyssey, and one was called the Iliad, and one was called Euripides, and they were all in Greek. Uncle Gideon loved them very much, and wouldn't let anyone go to the chest except Piers, who loved them too, especially the Odyssey, which was about ships and seaways and wonderful adventures.

Upstairs again was Aunt Deborah's and Uncle Gideon's chamber, and that had glass in the window too; and the room where Tamsyn and Beatrix slept in a big bed with dark-blue curtains and Littlest slept in a truckle bed with no curtains at all; and that room had no glass in the window. It was rather draughty when the wind blew, because you couldn't shut out the wind without shutting out the light as well.

Highest up of all, high under the eaves, among the stars and the winds of heaven, were the tiny cubby-holes that belonged to Meg the Kitchen and Piers and Giles and Timothy, and a long, low attic that ran all the length of the Dolphin House, with a window at one end looking across the river, and a window at the other end peering down into the street. There were boxes and bales stacked against the walls, barrels for storing apples in bran, an old side-saddle, and several quarter-staffs propped in a corner, creaking floorboards, and cobwebs festooned from the rafters, and an interesting smell of damp and mice and hidden secrets. This was supposed to be a place for storing things, but really and truly it was the Children's Kingdom, and they called it 'Kit's Castle'. Kit had started calling it that, when he was five years old; he had stood at the top of the stairs and shouted, 'I am Kit Caunter, and this is my castle'. And it had been Kit's Castle ever since. There was a big chest under one window, where the children kept all the things they had collected at odd times: some pieces of gay, worn-out cloth, and a king's crown of gilded pasteboard with the gilt beginning to wear off, a pair of wooden swords, and a sandal-wood box with a hunting scene carved on the lid, and a dried sea-horse that an old sailor had once given Kit, a pewter mug with a dint in it, and five peacock feathers, and a lot of other things. Giles kept his beetles and caterpillars up there too, in boxes with air holes in the lids. When it was wet or cold, so that they could not play in the narrow garden, or whenever they happened to feel like it, even if the sun was shining, they would scramble up the steep stairway that wound round and round its central post like the stripes round a barber's pole so that you were quite dizzy when you got to the top, and drag out all the delightful things in the chest and do whatever best pleased them, with no one to interfere.

Littlest never played with the others. He withdrew into a corner with his beloved Lammy, the white woolly lamb with gold spangles on its fleece and sharp tin legs, which Piers had brought him from last St. Bartholomew's Fair, to do strange and complicated things with bits of twine and twigs and scraps of pasteboard. Nobody ever knew what Littlest was doing, unless perhaps he was having battles; but whatever it was, it interested him very much, and he always kept the tip of his little pink tongue stuck out of the side of his mouth while he was doing it. Bunch generally sat by him, blowing his cheeks in and out and thumping his tail gently on the floor, and watching very carefully. There was only one thing Littlest would rather have had to play with than his twigs and bits of twine, and that was the bundle of peacocks' feathers out of the play-chest. He wanted and wanted those lovely jewel-bright feathers to play with, but the Almost-Twins would never let him have them, so that was that.

Beatrix and Giles did all sorts of interesting things up in Kit's Castle, and made all sorts of exciting make-believes; but at first Tamsyn found it very hard to join in, although they were quite willing to have her (in a condescending sort of way, that is). She had never played with other children before, and she didn't quite know how; besides, she always had to be the villain. She got rather tired of always being the villain, and once she actually said so; but Beatrix said scornfully, 'Don't be silly! You can't possibly be anything but the villain; you're too dark.'

And of course it was quite true, really. She was so very dark, with black eyes and a cloud of black hair and a berry-brown skin, and all the best villains *are* dark. And then Giles said loftily, 'Never mind, you do it quite well, considering. At least, you would if you'd only put a bit more heart into it.' So Tamsyn went on being the villain, and did her best to put a bit more heart into it.

Every morning after six o'clock breakfast, when Uncle Gideon and Piers had betaken themselves to the workshop, and Giles, with his dinner in one hand and his slate in the other, had gone dashing up the street to St. Paul's School, Beatrix and Tamsyn did lessons in the parlour with Aunt Deborah. They each had a hornbook tied on to their middles. This was a square of parchment sandwiched between two squares of horn to keep it clean, and it had a wooden handle to hold it by, so that it made quite a good battledore when you were not using it for lessons. At the top of each hornbook was written in large black letters:

'Christ's Cross be my speed
In all virtue to proceed.'

Then there were the numbers 1 to 10, and then the Lord's Prayer, and then the alphabet. They learned to spell from it, and did sums, and then they each wrote a copy, and after that they learned to play simple tunes on the clavichord; it had yellow ivory keys and a hawking scene on the back, and Aunt Deborah sometimes played on it to Uncle Gideon and the children in the evenings. Last of all, they did a little fine sewing, while Aunt Deborah read to them from the great Bible. They enjoyed that part of lessons very much, because Aunt Deborah had a lovely warm voice and always added little bits out of her own head to the Bible stories as she went along, so that afterwards one knew exactly the colour and trimming of Noah's Sunday doublet, and what David had had for breakfast on the morning he went out and killed Goliath.

After lessons they generally went out shopping, each with a basket on one arm and a little posy of herbs to sniff because the streets of London did not smell at all nice. Sometimes they did their shopping quite near at hand, but at other times they went right away past St. Paul's, whose spire was so high that it looked as though it must prick the floor of heaven, until they came to Cheapside. Tamsyn was always glad when they went to Cheapside, because it was so full and gay and busy. There were stalls all down both sides of the street, with awnings of blue and scarlet and emerald to shelter them from rain or sun, and inside, under the brilliant awnings, were everything from silver hawk-bells to copper preserving-pans, and larded guinea-fowls to frilly double primroses in pots. Cheapside was always full from end to end of people, gossiping, bargaining, counting their change or shouting that they had been robbed, or laughing at a friend who had slipped on a cabbage leaf; housewives and shopkeepers, country folk with shoes made of plaited straw, hurrying prentice lads, sailors from Billingsgate with gold rings in their ears, merchants bustling along in their furred gowns, children and dogs playing and fighting and stealing things off the stalls and sleeping in odd corners. All the hustle and noise and colour somehow comforted Tamsyn deep down inside, so that when she was there she forgot to feel homesick.

One morning, about three weeks after Tamsyn came to live in the Dolphin House, she and Beatrix went shopping with Aunt Deborah as usual. It was a blustery end-of-March day, with little patches of golden sunshine and little scurries of grey rain; and they put on their frieze cloaks (Beatrix's was dark green with a pale-green lining because of her red hair, and Tamsyn's was deep blue with an orange-tawny lining, rather like a kingfisher), and pulled the hoods well forward over their heads. Then they took their flat baskets in one hand and their posies of bee-balm and rosemary in the other, and went downstairs into the workshop. It was as nice as usual in the workshop, with its lovely smell of hot metal and oil and engraving acid, the ring and rasp of tools, and the forge fire filling the whole place with leaping shadows and red, flickering light. Timothy squinted at them in the most delightful way, rather like a bullfrog, when Uncle Gideon was not looking; but Piers was not there at all, because he had been sent on an errand to the other end of the City. Then Aunt Deborah came downstairs with her basket and posy, and they all went out into the street.

As soon as the door was closed behind them, Aunt Deborah stopped and looked at her list. 'Cloves,' she said, 'saffron for a cake, fine linen thread to mend father's best shirt; it must be because he's so thin that all the nobbly parts come through so quickly; other people don't wear out their shirts like that, I'm sure. Where was I? Oh yes, ginger, and fish for supper. That's all.' And she set off up the street, with Beatrix and Tamsyn following close behind her because there was not room to walk three abreast in the London streets without blocking the way and getting mixed up with the crowds of people all coming and going about their business in a great hurry. They went to the mercer's first, for the linen thread, and then to the spicer's for the cloves and saffron and ginger. The spicer's little dark shop smelt lovely: a sort of dark-brown smell made up of cloves and nutmeg, cinnamon and ginger, and sweet dried fruit and hundreds of other things. It came on to rain quite hard while they were there, and the spicer said they must wait until the shower was over, and his wife gave Beatrix and Tamsyn each a dried fig to eat while they waited. Tamsyn had never tasted a dried fig before, and she liked it very much.

Quite soon the sun came out again, and all the world sparkled silver-gilt, and the puddles in the street reflected joyous patches of blue sky until the wind ruffled them up into shivering silver ripples that could not reflect anything at all; and there was a rainbow curving above the far end of the street as they scurried along it towards Billingsgate to get the fish for supper, which was the last thing on Aunt Deborah's list.

Billingsgate was just as crowded as Cheapside, only here, instead of all the different things you could buy in Cheapside, were gleaming silver fish, with the spring sunshine turning them to gold: fish lying in piles on the cobbles, fish in great baskets, fish being loaded into carts, and the russet sails of the fishing-smacks and oyster-boats rising above the edge of the quay, and gulls everywhere, wheeling and crying above the heads of the people.

They went right along the quay until they came to the place where Aunt Deborah always bought her fish, just where Billingsgate suddenly stopped being a fish market and became a quay for shipping. That was the part of London that Tamsyn liked best. The tall warehouses reared their pointed gables against the sky, and the smell of fish faded into the mixed smells of rope and pitch, salt water and timber. There were crowds of seamen in red stocking-caps, and merchants, and bales of merchandise and coils of rope; and the tall ships of London Town were made fast alongside the wharves and jetties, or rode at anchor out in the stream. It was a little like being on Bideford Quay, although it was all so much bigger; same sort of ships, same sort of sailormen, same cobweb rigging high overhead, same flash and flicker of the river running by. Only this was the Thames instead of the Torridge; and when Tamsyn turned round and looked westward, there was London Bridge, with houses and shops built all along it, so that it was like a street on arches, instead of the narrow pack-bridge across the Torridge; and instead of the little bridge chapel where the yellow wagtails scuttled up and down the roof in summer, there was the tall spire of St. Mary of the Ferry standing up like a pointing finger above the higgledy-piggledy roofs of Southwark.

Tamsyn looked at London Bridge, and she looked at Aunt Deborah, and she looked again at the crowding masts and furled sails of the shipping, and she longed with a homesick longing to get near those ships. Aunt Deborah was busy choosing her fish, and Beatrix was helping her. They would never notice. She gave a little gasp of determination, and hitching up her basket and taking a firm hold on her posy of bee-balm and rosemary, she went boldly forward into the jostling crowds of the broad quay.

It was just after high tide, and one great ship was casting off from the quay-side with her sails already loosed, and Tamsyn squirmed and dodged and darted through the throng until she got close alongside, where she could watch all the lovely heartstirring bustle of departure as the ropes that held the great ship to the shore were cast off. Only one rope remained, made fast to her stern and to the quay quite near her bows, so that as the helm was put over, the current would carry her out into the stream; and even as

Tamsyn watched, the rope began to swing out, and the ship to drift away from the quay-side. Soon the sails would fill and she would drop down-river with the tide. Tamsyn wondered where she was going; to white ports along the coast of the blue Mediterranean, perhaps for ginger and silk and sandal-wood; or just across the narrow seas to bring back the red wine of Gascony; or even westward to the Golden Indies, as the *Joyous Venture* would sail in a year's time.

'Oh, if only I was a boy,' thought Tamsyn desperately. 'Then I could have sailed westward one day, too. Oh, if *only*——'

And then suddenly she saw Piers.

He was standing quite close by, but he had not seen her. He seemed to have forgotten the crowds coming and going all round him, and appeared to see nothing at all except the lovely ship swinging away from the quay as the last rope was cast off. He was watching her as though the only thing he wanted in the whole wide world was to be sailing with her.

Tamsyn had never seen anyone look quite like that before, and it made her feel queer and screwed-up in her inside, and somehow as though she ought not to be watching, and she was just going to watch the ship again, instead, when Piers looked round and saw her. His face went queer and still, and for a long moment they just stared at each other; then Piers shook his head in a way that she knew was meant to warn her against calling out to him, and next instant he had turned and plunged away into the crowd.

Tamsyn stood quite still, while you might have counted five, with her mouth and eyes very wide open, staring at the place where he had disappeared. Then she shut her mouth tight, and took one last look at the tall ship that was drifting farther and farther from the quay, and went back to Aunt Deborah and Beatrix.

They had finished buying the fish for supper, and were coming to look for her.

'Tamsyn,' said Aunt Deborah the moment she saw her, 'where *have* you been, you bad poppet? I thought you'd stolen off and run all the way back to Devon.' But she said it quite comfortably, as though she did not mean it. Aunt Deborah hardly ever did mean it when she said things like that. It made her very poor at scolding, though she could smack quite well when necessary.

'She was watching that ship,' said Beatrix officiously; 'the one that's just setting sail. I saw her. I expect she's queer about ships, like Piers used to be.'

But Tamsyn didn't say anything at all, and all the way home she was very thoughtful.

When she saw Piers again that evening at supper, she looked at him very carefully, to see if he looked just as usual; and he did. And he never said anything about having been at Billingsgate that day, so she didn't say anything about it either; but she went on being thoughtful.

2 *The 'Dolphin and Joyous Venture'*

Every year, about Easter, Uncle Gideon Caunter gave his craftsmen a day's holiday, and he and his family went down by the
river to Chelsea Meadows, and took their dinner with them.
Tamsyn had been told all about it quite soon after she came to live
in the Dolphin House, and as the day for the outing drew nearer
she was just as excited as the others. For days beforehand she
and the Almost-Twins spent their time hanging out of the windows

to make sure that it was not going to rain, and Aunt Deborah and Meg the Kitchen spent their time in baking pies and pasties, and Uncle Gideon spent his time just as though nothing stupendous was going to happen, and said that bread-and-cheese was all they needed, which exasperated Aunt Deborah so much that she gave him boiled mutton *without* prunes for supper two evenings running, because that was his least favourite supper.

On the very last evening grey clouds rolled up out of the west and it began to look like rain, and everyone was in despair; but the clouds passed in the night to rain somewhere else, and when the morning came it was a blue-and-golden one, with no clouds at all except tiny ones like curled golden feathers floating high, high against the blue. Tamsyn got up very early, and dressed herself in a great hurry, and so did Beatrix. They put on their leaf-green gowns that were generally kept for Sundays, with low square necks that showed the gathered and embroidered tops of their chemises, and grey worsted stockings clocked with scarlet, and sensible shoes. Then they dressed Littlest between them, in his russet-brown doublet and hose. Dressing Littlest was rather difficult, because he was so busy all the time and was always wanting to look out of the window or get under the bed or jump like a frog. Before Tamsyn came to live with them Aunt Deborah had dressed him herself, because Beatrix could not manage him very well, and his father did not like it if he came down to breakfast with his hose in wrinkles round his sturdy legs and his shirt hanging out behind. But Tamsyn and Beatrix together could manage him beautifully: they hitched up his hose and tucked in his shirt and brushed his red-gold hair into his eyes, and took him downstairs to have his face and hands washed at the well in the kitchen. Then they washed their own, and after that they were ready for breakfast and very hungry. Dressing Littlest always made them hungry—it was such hard work.

After breakfast there was such a hurrying to and fro and up and down that Bunch thought his family meant to go away for ever and leave him behind; and he sat down in the middle of the parlour and howled and howled and howled, so that everybody had to stop whatever they were doing to comfort him and assure him that they were only going for the day and anyway he was coming too.

At last everything was ready, and they set out.

The Dolphin House had a narrow garden behind it, which ended in a wall above the river. But it had not got its own steps down to the water, as some gardens had; and so the family had to go along the street a little way, and down a narrow alley to a flight of river steps at the far end, where the tilt-boat which Uncle Gideon had hired for the day would be waiting for them.

They went in triumphant procession: first Aunt Deborah in her best blue damask gown, holding Littlest by the hand, and Littlest clutching Lammy to his chest; then Piers and Uncle Gideon in their best broadcloth doublets, carrying the basket with the dinner in it between them. Then came the Almost-Twins side by side as usual. Giles had a tin trumpet, but Uncle Gideon had forbidden him to blow it until they were out of London, so he just strode along holding it to his mouth and breathing carefully through his nose, and only blew two accidental toots all the way. Lastly there was Tamsyn and Bunch. Tamsyn was glad to have Bunch to walk with; it wasn't quite so lonely as having to walk all by herself.

When they came to the river steps they found the tilt-boat waiting for them as arranged; a nice tilt-boat with red and blue paint on the gunwales and two watermen all complete. One of the watermen was young and pink, and the other one was old and hairy, but they both had friendly expressions. The tide was out, and the two lowest steps were wet and green and slippery, with long green weed fanning out on the water like mermaid's hair; and when Uncle Gideon had settled the dinner-basket with Littlest and Lammy on top of it, and came back for Aunt Deborah, he said, 'Be careful you don't slip.'

'You'll save me if I do, won't you, Gideon dear?' said Aunt Deborah, giving him a lovely smile because she loved outings and was sorry about the mutton without prunes two nights running; and she put her hand on his arm, and swept down the steps and into the tilt-boat like a queen entering her royal barge. Piers and Uncle Gideon saw the rest of the family in safely, including Bunch, and then stepped aboard themselves, and the watermen pushed off from the steps, and the outing had begun!

Tamsyn had never been in a Thames tilt-boat before, and she found it all very exciting, especially when she had wriggled well forward so that the tilt—which was a kind of hood—did not shut out any of the view. The boatmen bent to their oars, and the boat skimmed through the water, which slapped and whispered and sparkled along her sides. Past the Black Friars' Monastery they went, past tall houses crowding to the water's edge to watch their own reflections, and the lovely gardens of the Strand, threading their way among the river traffic of pleasure barges and grain barges and tilt-boats plying for hire, until they came opposite Whitehall Palace. Uncle Gideon said the King's Grace was at Greenwich, and so it was no use looking out for him; but they looked all the same, just in case. Then the boat carried them on, past Westminster, and more great houses with smooth green lawns to the water's edge and hedges of clipped yew and terraces full of the blue and golden flowers of spring. In one garden they saw a peacock strutting down a sloping lawn with all the jewelled eyes in the spread glory of his tail staring back at the sun, which reminded Littlest of the five peacock feathers in the play-chest in Kit's Castle, and made him quite sad for a minute or so. Once they passed a barge hung with rose and purple tapestries speeding up to Westminster, with a great lady sitting in the stern with a little dog in her lap, who barked at Bunch. So of course Bunch barked back so hard that Giles had to grab him by the tail to keep him from barking himself into the river.

Presently they came to open country, and at last the tilt-boat ran in under the steep bank, and everybody scrambled ashore. It was a lovely place. The river wound through low-lying meadows, and the shoots of the pollard willows along its banks were crimson with rising sap and bursting out into a haze of leaves that were like tiny silver-green candle-flames, and all the meadows were spread with a royal carpet of yellow irises and Mary-buds. Away across the fields Tamsyn could see the little village of Chelsea, half hidden behind poplar trees whose baby leaves fluttered gold in the sunshine; and far away to the north-east rose the towers and spires of London, looking like a city in a fairy-tale, not like the real-life workaday city that they had woken up and had their breakfasts in that morning. It was the first time Tamsyn had seen green meadows or heard lark-song since she came to live in the Dolphin House; and she wanted to kilt up her skirts and run, and run, and run, and never go back to London any more.

Then Giles began to blow joyful blasts on his tin trumpet, and Beatrix began to sing at the top of her voice:

'Lenten is come with love to town,
With blossoms and with birdés round,
And all bliss bringeth;
Day's-eyes in the dales,
Notes sweet of Nightingales
Which blithe song singeth.'

It was a very old song, so old that it had been made in the days when people still called daisies 'Day's-eyes', but it had a tune that sounded as new as the very newest Mary-bud in Chelsea Meadows. Tamsyn began to sing it too, and Giles still tootled blithely on his tin trumpet. But Littlest was not interested in music; he said very firmly, over and over again, 'Littlest wants his dinner. Littlest wants his dinner! *Littlest wants——*'

So they found a nice place under some alder trees, and Aunt Deborah uncovered the basket and spread a damask cloth on the grass, and began to take out all the things that she and Meg the Kitchen had made; and everybody sat down on the grass under the alder trees and had their dinner. There was a huge rook pie, cherry conserve pasties and pink-and-white ham smelling of herbs, and yellow marchpanes, and ridiculous little gingerbread men bright with gilt. Everybody ate a lot and talked a lot. At home it was 'Silence at meals' because of the children, but out here in the green meadows it was quite different; everyone could talk as much as they liked, and they did.

After they had eaten everything there was to eat, Aunt Deborah shook out the cloth and scattered the crumbs for the birds, and packed the basket up again, and everybody played Hot-cockles and Hoodman-blind to shake down the pies and pasties—even Uncle Gideon, who never played running-about games with the children on any other day of the year except at Christmas time. Presently, when their dinner was nicely shaken down, the party split up. Piers was the first to go; he wandered off downstream by himself—at least, he started by himself, but Littlest trundled after him, still clutching Lammy, and shouting, 'Piers, wait for Littlest. Piers, Littlest is coming too!' And so they disappeared together.

Beatrix watched him go, and tossed her head scornfully. 'Just look at Piers,' she whispered to Giles, 'mooning off like that! What's the good of having a brother if all he does is to moon off by himself when he could be jolly with the rest of us?'

'I s'pose he likes it,' said Giles. 'He can't help being queer and —and not like Kit.'

'I wish he *was* like Kit,' whispered back Beatrix, pretending to do something to her shoe. 'It was fun before Kit was drowned.'

They had been very careful not to let their mother hear what they were saying, but Tamsyn was close by, and she heard them quite plainly, and she thought Kit must have been a very wonderful person, because the Almost-Twins were always saying how far superior he was to Piers, and *she* thought Piers was very nice indeed; but she didn't say anything at all, because they were not speaking to her.

'Oh, Piers is all right,' said Giles, in a kindly, condescending sort of way. 'Let's you and me go and explore.' So they did, and Bunch went with them.

Uncle Gideon lay down under a blackthorn tree, with his hands behind his head, and thought how nice it was to have nothing to do; and Tamsyn went down to the river bank with Aunt Deborah, and helped her to gather great armfuls of yellow iris leaves for strewing the parlour floor when they got back. (Meg strewed fresh rushes and herbs on the parlour floor every week, camomile and hyssop and red-mint, but yellow iris leaves made the nicest strewing herb of all.)

Presently, when they had picked enough, Aunt Deborah went to sit beside Uncle Gideon, because she thought it would be nice to be lazy for a little while, too; and Tamsyn slipped away by herself and followed the river up-stream until she came over a little lift of ground to a place that seemed to have been made especially for her, and not for anyone else in all the world. It was a hollow with a tiny stream running through it to join the winding Thames. Willow and hazel and alder shut it off from the workaday world, and from edge to edge it was full of the clear singing gold of Mary-buds (marsh marigolds we call them nowadays), all except in one place beside the stream, where there was a tiny plot of fairy green as smooth as a dancing-floor, all ringed round with tall yellow flags like lamps kindled for a ball; a dancing-floor for the fairy-folk and lamps to light their revels when the blue spring twilight flowed over Chelsea Meadows. Tamsyn stood for a moment on the rim of the hollow, and then she kilted up her green kirtle and ran down through the golden cups of the Mary-buds to the little green dancing-floor beside the stream.

And what should one do with a dancing-floor but dance on it?

Tamsyn spread her skirts and danced until her hair flew out like a dark cloud round her head and her cheeks were pink as foxgloves under the brownness of her skin, and her sensible shoes might have been golden slippers made by the fairy shoemakers, they were so light upon the grass.

When she had danced until she was tired, she sat down on her heels in the very middle of the dancing-floor, and stayed quite still. She was not lonely any more; she was never lonely when she was by herself in the green out-doors, only when she was with other people whom she did not really belong to. And the little hollow was so friendly, just as though it had been waiting for her all along and was glad she had come. The stream ran by over its speckled stones, the sharp-scented watermint made a blue haze along its banks, and all around her the yellow flags were folding back their first petals to the sunshine, and high overhead larks sang in the blue—hundreds and hundreds of them, so that the whole sky seemed to shimmer with their song. Tamsyn sat as still as a little wild thing, a bright-eyed field-mouse or a baby rabbit, with the little hollow to keep her company, and felt quite, quite happy for the first time since she had said good-bye to her old home.

She sat there until at last the time came when she knew she must go back to the others. She did not want to go. She wanted to build a little hut on the edge of the dancing-floor and live there for ever, with the larks and the alder trees and the speckle-stoned streamlet for company; and she did not think the Good People would mind. But she knew that if she did not go back soon, someone would come to look for her, and she hated to think of anyone—even Piers, who was quite the nicest of the family—coming and finding her here in her lovely secret place.

So she got up and shook out her skirts, and climbed up through the wild irises and the golden Mary-buds, and left the hollow and the streamlet and the dancing-floor of fairy-green behind her. She did not pick any of the Mary-buds, because she never wanted to pick flowers; and she did not look back, because she had the oddest feeling that if she did, the hollow and the streamlet and the dancing-floor would not be there any more.

When Tamsyn got close to the place she had started from, she found that the whole family had come together again. Pretty Aunt Deborah in her blue gown was sitting under the starry blackthorn tree, and she seemed to be telling a story to the others, who were gathered round her to listen. They all looked so happy and comfortable together, and there was no room for Tamsyn, no room at all. She didn't belong to them; she didn't belong to anyone, now, in all the world. For a little while she just stood quite still, watching them; and all the lovely happiness of her tiny dancing-floor took wings and flew away and left her, and she felt shut out and more forlorn than she had ever felt before, with a dreadful sort of black misery beginning to ache deep down inside her, like being hungry, only a thousand times worse.

But at last Aunt Deborah looked up and saw her standing there, and waved to her, and called, 'Come along, Tamsyn my poppet,' and Tamsyn came slowly across the grass, and Piers made room for her between him and his mother, and smiled at her in his quiet, grave way that somehow made his ugly face look rather nice. So she sat down on her heels, and listened to the end of the story; but the misery went on aching deep down inside her, because she did not belong, and it was dreadful not to belong.

When the story was finished, they had the afternoon bread-and-raisins, and all the bits of marchpane and the gingerbread men that were left over from dinner, and quite soon after that it was time to go home because of Littlest's bedtime. So they went back to the place where the tilt-boat was waiting for them with the two watermen lounging on the bank with the remains of their dinner all around them, casting dice against each other in a lazy sort of way; and they all climbed aboard, and the watermen cast off and sent the tilt-boat skimming back through the water towards London.

Everybody was very nice to Tamsyn on the way home, because she seemed rather quiet; and Beatrix, who was a kind person when she was not too busy being Queen Catherine or someone out of the Bible, gave her half the lapful of Mary-buds that she had gathered. Tamsyn thanked her politely for the Mary-buds, and said, No, thank you, she hadn't eaten too much gingerbread, when Aunt Deborah asked her; and then she suddenly became so merry and laughed so much at the queer faces Giles had begun to pull, that everybody thought they had been quite mistaken about her being quieter than usual.

Little by little the river broadened, and the towers and spires

20

and steep roofs of London Town rose up along the banks; and the green meadows and the lark-song were left behind; and Littlest was sound asleep with his coppery head nidnodding against Aunt Deborah's shoulder long before they reached the river steps from which they had started out. He never woke up, even when they trooped ashore, with the lovely outing all over for another year; so they carried him home and put him to bed, and then they all had supper.

It was a nice supper, but somehow it turned dry and tasteless in Tamsyn's mouth, so that she could hardly swallow it. And when it was over, and the Almost-Twins had wandered into the garden because there was still a little sunshine left over from the day and they wanted to see how a thrush who had a nest in the quince tree was getting on, she went up to Kit's Castle, where there was no one to see her, and sat herself down on the children's play-chest under the window, and cried—and cried—and cried, for loneliness and homesickness, as though her heart would break.

She cried for a long time, huddled up in a small, despairing lump in the deep window-recess, and she was still crying as hard as ever when a voice close above her said, 'What's the trouble, old lady?'

Tamsyn jumped nearly out of her skin, and looked up; and then she saw that Piers was standing beside the play-chest and looking down at her, in an inquiring sort of way.

'What's the trouble, Tamsy?' he asked again.

Tamsyn swallowed hard, and blinked even harder, and said very firmly, 'Nothing, thank you.'

She did wish that Piers would go away. But Piers didn't go away. Instead he sat down on the play-chest and put an arm round her in a motherly sort of way, and said very kindly, 'Are you homesick? Is that it?'

Tamsyn tried to say she had a fly in her eye and that was all, thank you, but it was no use, the words would not come out straight; she tried dreadfully hard not to cry any more, but that was no use either. So she burst into a fresh flood of tears all down the front of Pier's Sunday doublet, and wept out the whole story in little bits between gulps and sobs and snuffles, while Piers made small, comforting noises and patted her on the back consolingly.

'Nobody wants m-me,' wept Tamsyn. 'I don't belong to n-nobody, and I am so m-miser-rubble. And today I found a little green —p-place, and I was happy there, and I wanted and w-wanted to stay— and when I came back you were all so—c-comfortable together, an' there wasn't any *room* for me.'

Piers went on patting her on the back. 'Poor old lady,' he said. 'Poor old lady.'

'N-nobody wants me,' wept Tamsyn despairingly. 'Nobody's gug-glad I've come; oh dear, oh dear!'

'Tamsy,' said Piers very firmly, 'I'm glad you've come. We all are; but if nobody else is—*I'm* glad you've come.'

Tamsyn was so surprised that she quite stopped crying and looked at him with one eye. 'Truly?' she asked.

'Truly,' said Piers.

She gave another sob, because when you have been crying very hard for a long time it is not easy to stop all at once; and Piers said anxiously, 'Tamsy, do stop it; you'll be sick if you go on like this.'

'I *am* stopping it,' said Tamsyn with dignity. 'I'm stopping it as f-fast as I can,' and she made a valiant effort and swallowed two or three more sobs and said, 'I've stopped now.'

'Good girl!' said Piers, and he fished in the breast of his doublet and pulled out a large kerchief and mopped her face with it, very carefully, drying in all the corners.

Tamsyn sat quite still to have her face mopped, with just an occasional snuffle and hiccough (she always got the hiccoughs when she had been crying), and then, without knowing quite how it happened, she found she was telling Piers all about Uncle Martin and Home. She told him about the pink and white convolvulus along the sunk lanes, and the high cliffs above the Atlantic where the peregrine falcons nested. She told him about the little grey house with golden lichen dappling its roof, and her own room under the eaves with the odd-shaped window through which she could see Lundy floating like a cloud far out to sea, as she lay in bed on summer evenings; and her own little garden in the corner of Grandmother's big one, where she grew pansies and parsley and small trees from the cherry stones and beech nuts and crimson sprouting acorns that she found in the autumn woods; and about the May tree at the bottom of the orchard. It was a very old May tree, and carved on its gnarled trunk were three names and a date that you could still read quite clearly although the bark had crept in over the edges of the letters: 'Gideon Caunter, Martin Caunter, Christopher Caunter. Anno Domini 1506', which had been put there nearly thirty years ago by Tamsyn's father and uncles, one fine summer afternoon when someone had given Uncle Gideon a new knife. Uncle Martin had told her all about it, and now she told Piers.

She told him how you could stand on the hill above the house and see the tall ships sailing out over the Bar and away beyond Lundy; and she told him about the *Joyous Venture*, which would be swifter and more beautiful than any ship of the Port of Bideford, when she was launched and sailed for the West Indies. All the dreadful lost-dog feeling of not belonging to anyone had somehow gone quite away, leaving a warm, comforted sort of feeling inside her instead. And Piers seemed so interested, and asked just the right questions at the right moment, and she talked on, and on and on, until she had talked herself quite empty. She even told him about wanting to be a boy so that she could be a sailor when she was older, and have adventure and sail the seas of all the world, which was a thing she would never have dreamed of telling any of the other Dolphin House people.

Piers didn't say a word while she was telling him about wanting to go to sea, and when she had quite finished, he said, 'I know. I've always wanted to go to sea, too.'

And Tamsyn said, 'Oh! was that why you were watching that ship at Billingsgate?' And then she wondered if she ought not to have mentioned it. People are queer sometimes about not liking things mentioned.

But Piers didn't seem to mind at all. He only said, 'Yes, that was it. By the way, Tamsy, thanks for not mentioning it to anyone. If it had been Beatrix who saw me, she'd have told the whole family.'

Tamsyn thought for a little while. Uncle Gideon didn't look the sort of person who would not let you go to sea if you wanted to, but she supposed he must be, after all. So she suggested hopefully, 'I s'pose you couldn't run away?'

Piers laughed, but kindly, and said, 'No, I'm afraid I couldn't do that.' He stopped for a moment, and then he said, 'You see, Father's a very good armourer—about the best in London— and the shop means a lot to him: not only the shop, I mean, but making beautiful things; armour and weapons are like jewels and paintings to Father. Kit was to have joined him in the shop, and taken it on when Father was old. Kit always wanted that, as I always wanted to go to sea; but of course after he was drowned I had to try to take his place. Father would let me go if I asked him, but it isn't as though Giles cared a straw about the armoury, and anyway, I'm the eldest, so it really had to be me. I couldn't ever ask Father to let me go.'

'N-no,' said Tamsyn, 'I s'pose not.' But she said it rather doubtfully.

And Piers said, 'Oh, I don't expect I'll mind a bit when I'm old like Father. And I'm good at making things. I'll be a good armourer one day, you'll see. I'll make armour as light and strong and beautiful as the armourers of Nuremberg and Milan. I'll forge sword-blades of blue steel that you can bend in a circle with one finger, and damascene them with gold and silver so that people will buy my blades, instead of sending to the swordsmiths of Toledo.'

'Oh,' said Tamsyn, and then, 'how nice.' But she knew that Piers was only talking to comfort himself; so she said, 'Please— perhaps one day something *'strordinary* will happen, so you'll be able to go to sea after all.'

Piers said, 'Perhaps.' And then he got up off the play-chest and stood rocking gently on his heels and staring out of the window away across the river—which was all running gold in the sunset light—and talking very fast indeed, while Tamsyn sat quite still and watched him with her mouth and eyes very wide open. He had gone quite white across the bridge of his nose, so that the freckles stood out blacker than ever. That always happened to Piers when he minded very deeply about anything. But somehow he didn't seem ugly any more, in spite of his freckles and his ears. He didn't seem a bit like the quiet, workaday Piers at all, because the exciting part of him that Tamsyn had been so sure was there, hidden underneath where it did not show, was suddenly shining through. He talked of new seas to be sailed and new lands to be discovered and explored, and how one day English seamen would sail round the Cape of Storms and see the glories of Cathay, and westward to explore the wonders of the New World. How the Portuguese had had all the trade with India in their hands for five hundred years, and the Spaniards were trying to claim for themselves the Americas and all the trade routes to the west; but how the day was coming when the English would be masters of the seas, and the trade routes would be free to the shipping of all the nations, and there would be no blue water from Mexico to Cathay, and Cathay round again to the Gulf of Darien, that was not sailed by English ships and English seamen.

Then quite suddenly he stopped talking, and stood looking down at Tamsyn in the last golden light of the sunset; and he said rather gruffly, 'You'll not tell about all this, will you, Tamsyn? You're good at secrets.'

And Tamsyn slid off the toy-chest and stood very straight, with her hands folded in front of her, and stared up at him. 'I wouldn't tell a single *word*,' she said, 'not if they cut me in little bits, I wouldn't.'

Piers went on looking down at her as though he were making quite sure that he could trust her. Then he said, 'Have you ever seen a chart of the New World?'

'No,' said Tamsyn.

'Would you like to?'

'Please, yes,' said Tamsyn. 'Oh, *please,* yes.'

'Wait here, then,' and he turned and went away down Kit's Castle into the shadows that had begun to gather at the far end, and disappeared into the cubby-hole which he shared with Giles. In a little while he came back, carrying something rolled up in one hand, and a flaring rushlight in a brass pricket in the other, and the long attic changed from grey to golden at his coming.

'I brought a candle, because it's getting too dark to see properly,' he said, putting the pricket down on the top of an apple-barrel.

Tamsyn bundled across the creaking floor into the golden glow of the rushlight where Piers was sitting on his heels unrolling the rolled-up something; and she sat down on her heels too, beside him, and folded her hands in her leaf-green lap, and looked at him with her head a little on one side, like a puppy that hopes you are going to throw a ball for it. Tamsyn always looked like that when she was interested. Piers finished unrolling the something and laid it down flat and put all the things in his wallet on to the corners to keep it from rolling up again.

Then he said, 'Look, Tamsyn.'

And Tamsyn looked.

It was a most lovely chart. There were both the Americas joined together like a pair of spectacles, with clear blue sea lapping all round them. Places were marked on the land; Brazil, which Master William Hawkins of Plymouth had explored only four years ago; and Peru, and Darien, and many more. There were broad rivers and wide plains, chains of snow-capped mountains, and people in strange bird head-dresses, black bears and milk-white deer fleeing through forests of pointed trees whose branches were full of gay, long-tailed birds, fire-breathing serpents, and little men with bows and arrows in their hands, and their heads set in the middle of their chests. The land was lovely, but the sea was lovelier. There were little, scalloped waves in the sea, and the tiny, jewel-bright islands of the West Indies, with names that seemed to sing themselves like a rhyme, when Piers read them over to her, very quietly—Cuba and Jamaica, Hispaniola, Tobago, Marguerite, Grenada. There was the golden sun in one corner and the silver moon in another, and a queer, complicated ,cross-shaped pattern with its four points marked N, S, E, and W. There were sea-serpents too, and little gay dolphins among the waves; and, loveliest of all, there was a ship—bigger than the sun and moon, but hardly as big as a walnut shell, and Tamsyn's heart went out to her the moment she saw her. She was such a gallant little ship, with small, proud castles, and a tiny blue dolphin under her bowsprit for a figure-head, and her bulwarks were gay with painted shields not so big as Tamsyn's little finger-nail, and her pennants streamed scarlet and blue from her mastheads, and her sails were full of wind as she sped over the scalloped waves towards the green-and-golden shores of the New World.

Tamsyn looked at everything in the golden glimmer of the rushlight; but most of all she looked at the proud little ship. 'Did you make the chart?' she whispered at last.

'Sebastian Cabot made it first,' said Piers. 'Only much bigger, of course, and without the place-names; and quite a lot of the rich merchants have copies of it. Master Roger Whitcome has one, and he let me copy it myself, in the evenings after school.

I—I thought I should need it, you see. It was before Kit was drowned.'

Tamsyn looked up at Piers and gave her head a small, sorry shake. And then she looked down again at the lovely, sparkling little ship. Somehow she didn't want that ship to have been made by Sebastian Cabot, though he *was* such a great seaman and had helped to discover the West Indies. So she said beseechingly, 'And the little ship?'

'I made the *Dolphin* for myself,' said Piers.

'You've given her topgallant sails,' said Tamsyn.

And Piers looked up at her quickly, and said, 'What do *you* know about topgallant sails, Baby?'

'The *Joyous Venture* is going to carry them,' explained Tamsyn. 'Uncle Martin says one day every ship will carry topgallant sails. Did you call her *Dolphin* because of the nice little dolphins in front of the house?'

'In a way,' said Piers. 'But I think I should have called her *Dolphin* anyway; there's something exciting and joyful and gloriously adventurous about a dolphin. You see what I mean?'

Tamsyn saw exactly what he meant, and she said: 'It's really just the same as Uncle Martin calling *his* ship the *Joyous Venture!*'

'Yes,' said Piers, in a quick sort of way. And then he said 'Ye-es,' again, in a considering sort of way, and took a little bit of sharpened lead out of his wallet, and said, 'we'll give her a new name, and write it under her, for a secret between you and me. It's rather a long one; but lots of ships have names just as long, like the *Peter and Pomegranate* and the *Catherine Bonaventure*.' And he drew a little scroll with a flourish at both ends, under the ship, while Tamsyn leaned forward breathlessly to watch him, and in the scroll he wrote very carefully, '*Dolphin and Joyous Venture*'.

'There,' he said, when it was done. 'I'll paint it in properly later on.'

Tamsyn said very softly, '*Dolphin and Joyous Venture*. It's the beautifullest name!'

And the little ship seemed to like her new name, too, and all her gay pennants fluttered in the fluttering candle-light, and the little dolphin under the bowsprit arched his back even more joyously than before.

Then Piers began to tell Tamsyn about the New World. People did not know very much about the Americas in those days, because so few people had been there yet, and that was what made it all so wonderfully exciting. There might be anything—simply *anything* —in those great hidden lands: cities of gold for golden Kings and Queens and golden Priests of the Sun, new races of white people, mountains whose tops pricked the starry sky, dragons and salamanders and snow-white unicorns. Nobody knew. The few people

26

who had been there, just as far as the borders, had brought back stories; and the people who hadn't been there at all, listened to them and made up more for themselves without quite knowing that they were making them up, and so the stories grew more and more wonderful and fantastic. Piers was good at stories, and when his heart was in anything he could always make it come alive for other people, if he wanted to. He made the New World come so alive for Tamsyn that she seemed to be on the deck of the ship no larger than a walnut shell, sailing over blue seas capped with little frilled white waves and full of leaping dolphins and rainbow-winged flying fish, into the Golden West. As it grew darker, even the shadows seemed to be crowding out from the corners of Kit's Castle, to throng round the edge of the candle-shine and sit on their heels and listen because they liked stories too; and after a while a tiny, russet-furred mouse crept out from behind the old side-saddle, and sat up to listen among the shadows, with his whiskers twitching and his eyes bright as stars.

But Tamsyn didn't see the mouse, or the shadows; she was off and away with Piers, following broad rivers and climbing tremendous ranges of blue mountains in search of the unknown—hidden lands, golden cities, fresh trade for England. Great trees swept high above their heads, with strange birds of white and pink and crimson darting and calling among the flowering branches, while the *Dolphin and Joyous Venture* lay waiting in deep bays for their return.

Presently, as if from a very long way off, she heard Aunt Deborah calling, 'Tamsyn, where are you? Bedtime, poppet!' And the bright birds and the rushing rivers were gone in a flash, and Tamsyn was back in Kit's Castle, sitting on her heels in the yellow glow of the rushlight, beside Piers, with the lovely chart spread out before them, and Piers was looking at her in his quiet, half-smiley way. The shadows stole back to their corners, and the mouse gave a whisk of his tail and was gone down his hole behind the old side-saddle before anyone knew that he had been there at all; and one silver star was hanging low out of a clear green sky to look in at Piers and Tamsyn and see what had interested them so much. For Kit's Castle was very near the stars, especially when people made magic in it.

'Tamsyn!' called Aunt Deborah again; and Tamsyn gave a little sigh, and a little wriggle, and called back, 'Coming, Aunt Deborah,' and got up. 'I must go,' she said sadly.

Piers rolled up the map and uncurled his long legs and got up too, giving his shoulders a little shake, as though he were shaking off the magic that he had made. 'Good-night, Tamsy,' he said.

Tamsyn bobbed him a good-night curtsy. 'It was lovely, Piers. And may I see the little ship again one day?'

Piers gave her a grave little bow in return for the curtsy. 'Of course,' he said. 'Are you not her part-owner?'

'Am I?' said Tamsyn. 'How *nice*.' And then she smiled suddenly, and said, 'Good-night,' and 'Thank you,' and pattered away down the circular stairway to Aunt Deborah and bed.

3 *May Day and Morris Dancers*

Tamsyn was a much happier person after the evening when the *Dolphin and Joyous Venture* got her name; and she was not nearly so homesick. Telling Piers about it had made all the difference, and she did not feel lonely or un-belonging any more, because she had made a friend and had a secret to share with him. Quite soon she began to feel that she belonged to the rest of the family too, which was a very comfortable thing to feel. Then she began to like London; it was not like her own dear countryside, of course; but it was nice, all the same.

In those days cities were not at all like they are now. They were small and compact and cosy, like a tit's nest. The houses were cuddled close together inside their city walls, with the towers of their cathedrals standing over them to keep them safe from harm. London was like that. As you came towards it, up the Strand from Westminster or over the meadows from Hampstead, you could see the towers and spires and steep roofs of the City rising above its protecting walls as gay as flowers in a flower-pot; and when you had passed through the gates (there were eight fine gates to London Town), the streets were narrow and crooked and very dirty, but bright with swinging shop-signs and hurrying crowds. And the shops under the brilliant signs were as gay as fairground booths, with broidered gloves and silver hand-mirrors, jewels to hang in ladies' ears, baskets of plaited rushes, coifs of bone lace, wooden cradles hung with little golden bells for wealthy babies. Other shops sold the rare and lovely things from overseas that were still new to the English people —Venetian goblets as fine as soap-bubbles, pale eastern silks, strange spices for rich men's tables, and musk in little flasks for people to make themselves smell nice. But if you wanted ordinary things, such as food or preserving pans, you went to Cheapside or some other market; and if you wanted herbs you went to the herb market, which was really one of the loveliest places in London, because most flowers and green things counted as herbs in those days.

The street of the Dolphin House was one of the nicest streets in

London. It was a very busy street, full of a great coming and going that went on all the daylight hours, so that there was always something to watch from the windows. Perhaps that was why the windows of the Dolphin House always looked so interested. Brown-clad monks, and church carvers and candle-makers, merchants and yet more merchants, and jewellers and silversmiths, and sailors everywhere—more sailors every day, it seemed to Tamsyn. All these came and went along the street, and sometimes a great lord would ride by on a tall horse, or a lady with winged sleeves of golden gauze and servants running ahead to clear the way for her. Strolling players often passed that way, too, on their way from Ludgate to the Fountain Tavern, where they acted their plays; and Morris Dancers, or a performing bear led by a little boy, or a man with a cadge of hawks for sale. Once a baker who had sold short-weight bread was drawn through the street sitting on a hurdle with the short-weight loaf tied round his neck, and half the little boys of London running behind in a joyful sort of way and throwing things. Oh, it was a very exciting street, and as the weeks went by, Tamsyn began to like it very much indeed.

There was a great coming and going in the Dolphin House too. All through the day-time people came to buy a sword or order a pair of mail gauntlets or perhaps even a whole suit of armour; great lords of the Court, and squires who were not great at all, and once the Lord High Admiral of England. And in the evening, when the working day was over, the other Master Craftsmen and merchants who were friends of Uncle Gideon's would often call in. They would sit round the polished table in the parlour and talk of Florentine velvets and damascened sword-blades and trade routes, the glories of the New World, and the demand for cinnamon. On such evenings Piers would sit near by, if he could manage it without being noticed, and listen, with his ugly face cupped in his hands, his eyes looking as though he was seeing things a long way off.

Well, so the spring drew on, and the quince tree at the bottom of the Dolphin House garden uncurled new green leaves that were like jets of emerald flame in the sunshine, and it was May Day.

Tamsyn woke up in the great bed with the blue curtains which she no longer minded sharing with Beatrix, while it was still quite dark on May Day morning, and heard two people creeping downstairs very stealthily in their stockinged feet. Just for a moment she held her breath and tingled all over. Then she remembered that it was May Day morning, and Piers and Timothy would be going out to bring home the May! So she began to breathe again, but she went on tingling all over because it was so exciting to feel that it was May Day. She did wish that she was going with Piers and Timothy and all the other people who would be streaming out to the woods and fields to see the sunrise and bring home the May. She could *not* think how Beatrix could go on sleeping like a dormouse, when it was May Day morning, and was just wondering whether or not she would shake her to wake her up, when suddenly she found that she had been to sleep again herself and the sun was poking golden fingers slantwise across the window.

It was a lovely morning, with a holiday feeling in the air that made Littlest even more difficult to dress than usual, because he wanted to jump like a frog *all* the time, instead of only now and then, and kicked joyously while Tamsyn was trying to brace up his hose. But they got him dressed at last, and just as they had finished, they heard a great noise of singing and shouting in the street.

'It's the May!' squealed Beatrix. 'They're bringing home the May.' And they all ran to the window and leaned out, the girls keeping a firm hold on Littlest's doublet to make sure he didn't fall into the street on his head.

There was a great throng of people pouring up the street in their gayest holiday clothes, shouting and singing as they came, and carrying great branches of flowering May and armfuls of bluebells and golden Mary-buds, so that the whole street seemed full of the spring and sunshine and happiness. On they came, laughing, singing, shouting and waving their flowering branches, and at each door in the street people dropped out of the throng and began to set up the May branches above the lintel.

'They're almost here,' shrieked Beatrix. 'Let's go down and meet them.' And next instant Giles came cascading downstairs from Kit's Castle, yelling and whooping, with Bunch barking at his heels, and they all dashed down into the workshop together, hauling Littlest with them.

They got to the front door and tore it open just as the lovely cavalcade came dancing past, and all the narrow street was full of laughter and tossing flowers and swirling skirts, and Littlest began to prance joyfully in the doorway, while the girls held tight to his hands. Then Piers and Timothy dropped out of the tail of the throng, each carrying a great branch of May thick with creamy blossom, and Tamsyn and Littlest and Bunch and the Almost-Twins all ran out to help them decorate the Dolphin House doorway.

After that, the day seemed depressingly ordinary for a bit; work went on much as usual in the workshop, and Beatrix and Tamsyn had to do their lessons, and Giles went very unwillingly to school, and after dinner Uncle Gideon went out on business taking Timothy with him. But quite soon after that, Aunt Deborah said she had run out of saffron and they must go shopping and get some more. She had not really run out of saffron at all; there was plenty in the blue earthenware jar with yellow and white flowers on it in the store cupboard; but Aunt Deborah, in spite of her lovely tall figure and high-piled hair, was not really a very grown-up person, and she wanted to see the merry-makings quite as much as the children did.

So she and Beatrix and Tamsyn and Littlest all set out. Aunt Deborah was the only one with a basket, because one basket is enough when you are only going to buy an ounce of saffron and don't really mind whether you buy it at all.

London was very gay and pretty that afternoon. A great many people seemed not to be working because of it being May Day, and there were crowds everywhere, in their holiday clothes, and holiday moods to match, laughing and shouting, singing and quarrelling, while their children and dogs played and fought all across the narrow streets. And every house they passed, from the great mansions of the richest folk to the little hovels of the poorest ones, was decked out with branches of hawthorn above the door. Some of the May branches had knots of spring flowers tied to them, some were sparkling with silver ribbons, some had only their own scented curds of blossom for beauty; but they were all lovely.

They bought the saffron at the spicer's, and then they decided they would go on just a little farther, before they turned home. Almost at once they met a man selling little gingerbread figures and striped sugar pigs; and Aunt Deborah said they could each have one, because of it being May Day, and she would have one too. So they each chose a sugar pig, and Beatrix put hers in her hanging pocket, because she was being Catherine of Aragon just then and felt it a little beneath her royal dignity to eat sugar pigs in the street. But nobody else had any dignity, and so they sucked joyfully. Tamsyn's pig was striped pink and green.

Then a swirl of music rose in the distance, shrill and sweet and coming nearer; and people came running to their doors and windows. ''Tis the Morris Dancers!' cried someone, and everyone took up the cry. 'The Morrissers! Way for the Morrissers!' People pressed back against the walls of the houses, and squashed together in doorways and climbed on to window-sills and shop counters, all with their necks craned to look for the May dancers. Aunt Deborah picked Littlest up so that he should have a good view, while Beatrix and Tamsyn wriggled between a stout butcher in a blue smock and an old woman with a basket of spring cabbages on her arm, so that they, too, had a good view. The lovely, merry music came nearer and nearer, with swirling pipes and jingling bells; and then round the corner of the street came the Morris Dancers, led by their musicians with pipes and tabors, and all a-ring and a-chime and a-jingle with the little silver bells on their arms and legs and round their waists.

First danced Maid Marian, who was the May Queen, too, for she wore a golden crown. She carried a crimson carnation in one hand, and her gown was purple and her kirtle green and her sleeves pink as May blossom; and Robin Hood danced beside her, all in green, with his bow in one hand and a gay peacock's feather in his bonnet. Then the Fool, all in red and yellow, with cock's comb flaunting and asses' ears swinging on his fantastic hood, and a stick with a carved wooden fool's head on top of it in his hand; and then Friar Tuck, with his habit hitched up to show his red stockings and the bells around his ankles. There was Scarlet, too, and Stukely, and Little John—all Robin Hood's men; and Jack-in-the-Green, who was a man bound round with green branches, so that he looked like a bush dancing along the street; and Tom Piper, with a feather in his crimson cap and a long wooden sword at his hip. And last of all came the Hobby-Horse, capering along behind the rest, a lovely, bright pink pasteboard horse with golden trappings and a rider in a cloak that was half blue and half yellow, whose feet appeared under the trappings, doing the most wonderful and complicated steps imaginable. On they went, dancing with queer, jerky steps that set their silver bells chiming like all the bells of Elfland; and behind them came a jostling, boisterous throng of girls and children, and prentice lads who should have been at work, and little boys who should have been at school, all out to enjoy themselves.

Tamsyn longed to kilt up her skirts and go with them, following the shrill Morris Music, which made her feet dance just to hear it; but Aunt Deborah said, 'Now we really must be getting home. Come along, poppets,' and she put Littlest on his feet and shooed them all off down the street in the direction of home. And the jiggiting music and the jingling of the Morris bells died away behind them in the distance.

But they had gone but a very little way when there began to be a new kind of noise in the City: an angry noise, quite a long way behind them, and above the uproar Tamsyn could hear a sudden cry of 'Clubs! Clubs!'

'Oh, deary me!' said Aunt Deborah, beginning to hurry a little. 'There's always trouble with the prentices on May Day, but it doesn't usually start as early as this.'

She had hardly finished speaking when the crowds in the street suddenly grew thicker than ever, as tall prentice lads came pouring out of shop doorways and went shouldering their way through the people in the direction of the distant shouting. They all carried stout cudgels, and looked very pleased and happy; and as they went they took up the cry, 'Clubs! Clubs!'

'Thank goodness we are nearly home,' said Aunt Deborah. 'Tamsyn, do come along, and stop looking behind you. You won't see anything interesting—at least, you won't if I can help it.'

'Clubs! Clubs!' shouted the shouldering prentices joyfully, and then, as word was passed back through the crowds, 'Rescue Ned

Buckle! Rescue Guildersleeve's prentice! Clubs! Clubs! Clubs!'

'I wonder whether it's a battle with the Watch or only between two lots of prentices,' said Beatrix. 'I *do* hope it's the Watch.'

'Well, whichever it is,' said Aunt Deborah, towing Littlest along by the hand rather faster than he wanted to go, 'our two won't be in it. Timothy is with Father at the other end of town, and Piers is much too quiet and steady.'

For a little while nobody answered her, and then Beatrix announced tragically to no one in particular, 'It's so *mortifying* to have a brother who stays at home when they're calling "Club" in the street. Kit would have gone at once. *He liked fighting.*'

Aunt Deborah said, 'Piers is a very good brother for anyone to have. Who drew pictures for you when you were ill, you nasty little girl? And who mends your things when you break them? Littlest, my lamb, *will* you pick your feet up. Besides, one fighter in a family is quite enough, and I'm sure there's hardly a week goes by that Giles doesn't come home from school with a black eye or a torn jerkin.'

But Beatrix only stuck her haughty nose in the air, and muttered, 'I don't care! *I'd* not stay at home working, while the other prentices were out fighting the Watch.'

'If you say another *word,* Beatrix Caunter,' shrieked Tamsyn, suddenly turning bright pink with fury, 'I'll hit you with my sugar pig—and it's all sticky.'

'Children! Children! Stop it at once,' ordered Aunt Deborah, while a fresh burst of shouting arose in the distance: 'Clubs! Clubs! Rescue Ned Buckle!'

'Littlest go,' said Littlest, and made a dive in the direction of the shouting.

Aunt Deborah dropped the basket and grabbed him by the skirts of his doublet. 'Littlest *not* go,' she said.

Then a queer thing happened; for Littlest, who was never cross or upset, sat down with a thump on the cobbles, and shut his eyes and opened his mouth and burst into a roar of tears. 'Oh, deary me!' said Aunt Deborah, quite comfortably. 'Tamsyn, pick up my basket and carry it.' And she scooped Littlest up from the cobbles, still yelling and with a face as scarlet and crumpled as a poppy-bud, tucked him under her arm and set off for home once more. Littlest was making so much noise that everybody turned round to stare at them as they passed, but Aunt Deborah did not seem to be at all put out. If you can imagine someone-in-a-stained-glass-window-with-the-sun-shining-through-it carrying a bawling little boy under one arm and the remains of a striped sugar pig in the other hand, that is exactly how Aunt Deborah looked.

They were in a narrow back-alley at the time, and in a little while they came out into a street, and the first thing they saw was

Timothy dashing up it as fast as his long legs would carry him, in the direction of the battle.

'Look!' cried Beatrix and Tamsyn together, quite forgetting their quarrel in their surprise. 'There's Timothy!'

'Oh, my goodness gracious me! He must have given Father the slip,' said Aunt Deborah. 'Ah well, he can but go to gaol for the night, and I daresay he will have plenty of company.'

When they got home, there was no sign of Piers.

'Us heard them calling "Clubs" in the streets, and off he went with the biggest mallet,' old Caleb the swordsmith told them.

Beatrix and Aunt Deborah stared at him with their mouths open, and even Littlest stopped yelling.

'But he's always so quiet,' gasped Aunt Deborah, putting Littlest down with a thump that was almost like dropping him. 'He's never done such a thing before!'

'There hasn't been no prentice riots this end of the town since he left school, Mistress,' said Caleb, 'and 'tis often the quiet ones as makes the best fighters.'

'And of course you didn't think to stop him?'

Old Caleb shook his head. 'Nay, Mistress, we was all prentices ourselves once.'

Aunt Deborah sat down on a clean space at the end of one of the work-benches and folded her hands in her lap. 'Timothy has given the Master the slip,' she said serenely, 'for we saw him just now. I expect they'll both go to gaol, and *I* shall go distracted, and you can all come and visit me in Bethlehem Hospital. That will be so nice.'

And at that moment the street door opened again, and Uncle Gideon came in. He shut the door behind him, looked at his family and his workmen, and said in a very matter-of-fact sort of way, 'Ah, I take it Piers is off, too.'

But when Giles came home a little later, and Beatrix told him the extraordinary news, he was not at all matter of fact about it. He whistled in a very rude and astonished sort of way, and said condescendingly, 'Poor old Piers! He'll get chopped into little bits by that crowd—I don't believe he knows how to hit anybody.'

Then Littlest was put to bed, and soon after that the family sat down to supper, and as Piers and Timothy had not come home, Aunt Deborah put some by for them, without mentioning it to Uncle Gideon.

But when supper was over and cleared away, and the Vesper bell was ringing from the Black Friars' Monastery, and still there was no sign of them, Aunt Deborah went to the open window, and stood looking down into the crowded street. 'I wonder where those two wicked boys have got to,' she said, not worried exactly, but just a little anxious. 'Surely they should be back by now.'

Uncle Gideon glanced up from the book he was reading, and said, 'Perhaps they are in gaol. Quite a lot of prentices will be, by this time, I expect. I shouldn't worry if I were you, my dear.'

At this, Beatrix flung her arms round her mother's waist and cried tragically, 'Piers is in gaol, and they'll hang him in the morning. I know they will—or perhaps he's weltering in his gore, and I *scorned* him.'

But at that moment a new uproar started, faint at first, but coming nearer—a great noise of shouting and the faint shrill music of pipes and tabors. 'Here come the Morris Dancers!' cried someone in the street below, and, so fast that it seemed like magic, heads came poking out of windows and people came thronging out of doorways, all laughing and eager. 'The Morrissers! The Morrissers!'

The Dolphin House children all rushed to the window and scrambled on to the cushioned sill, leaning so far out that if they had leaned any farther they would all have fallen into the street. Luckily by that time the crowd was so thick that they would not have been at all likely to hurt themselves if they had, because a crowd is much softer to fall on than cobbles. Even Uncle Gideon got up, with one finger marking the place in his book, and came to stand in the deep oriel window to look out over the heads of his family.

'Here they are!' shouted Giles. 'I say, they've got torches.'

And they had. There was still some sunlight caught among the roof-tops, but the blue shadows were just beginning to gather in the street below, so that the torches shone like so many dandelions as they came bobbing along between the houses, and the golden crowns and silver bells of the dancers sparkled and shimmered with little flecks of coloured light in the most entrancing way. They were the same Morris Dancers that Tamsyn had seen that afternoon, but something very exciting seemed to have happened to them since then. They had a ragged and rather battered look about them, and Maid Marian had lost her carnation and her crown, and Jack-in-the-Green had lost all his leafy branches except one, which wagged exultantly behind him like a tail. But they were dancing more joyously than ever, in the cock-a-hoop sort of way that a conquering hero might dance on the way home from a battle, and they seemed to be singing and cheering a good deal, and they carried the Fool shoulder high among them. The Fool was shouting, 'Cock-a-doodle doo! Cock-a-doodle-doo-o-o! Who broke the Alderman's head?' Robin Hood was holding an imaginary hunting-horn to his mouth and winding the most tremendous blasts on it; and altogether they had the look of a Triumphal Procession that is really enjoying itself.

There were a great many prentices in the procession, milling along just as triumphantly as the Morris Dancers, and singing and thumping their friends on the head in the most cheerful way; more and more and more prentices, until it did not seem possible that there could be so many in all London Town. And right at the hindmost tail of the procession swaggered two figures which the Dolphin House family knew.

'It's Piers!' shrieked Beatrix.

'It's Piers and Timothy!' yelled Giles.

'Go and bring those two up to me,' said Uncle Gideon.

The two figures dropped out at their own front door, and next instant Tamsyn and the Almost-Twins and Bunch had rushed from the room and gone cascading higgledy-piggledy downstairs to meet them. At the bottom of the stairs it was rather dark, and everybody got muddled up together so that nobody knew quite who it was they were falling over; but they got themselves sorted out at last, and climbed upstairs again into the parlour, where Aunt Deborah and Uncle Gideon were waiting for them.

Then they all stood still and looked at each other. Timothy's face seemed quite all right, but his jerkin was ripped off one shoulder; and Piers had a purple bruise all along his cheek-bone and a split lip. But they both had an air of modest triumph about them.

Uncle Gideon looked at Timothy's shoulder and Piers' face in a way that made them wriggle, and said, 'Now that you have thought fit to return, Piers and Timothy, may I ask what you have to say for yourselves? Timothy first.'

Timothy squirmed slightly inside his ragged clothes, and said, 'Well, sir, it—it just—sort of—happened.'

'I see,' said Uncle Gideon, 'Piers, have you anything to add to the very detailed account of your proceedings with which Timothy has just favoured us?'

Piers said, 'Well, sir, the Watch got one of Master Guildersleeve's prentices for cracking Alderman Branby's head with his fool's-head stick—he was the Fool in the Morris Dance, you know. He said Alderman Bransby had taken off his cap to scratch his head, and when he saw his bald head shining in the sun he couldn't resist it. Only he hit rather harder than he meant to, and Alderman Bransby didn't like it.'

'No,' said Uncle Gideon. 'I can imagine that he might not. Go on.'

'Well, so the Watch got hold of him and were going to put him in the pillory, and the prentice who was Robin Hood led the others to the rescue at once, and a brush started, and they were calling Clubs in the street.'

'And so you took my best mallet and went to answer the call.'

'Yes, sir, but I've brought it back safely,' said Piers.

Uncle Gideon ignored this, and said, 'I never thought that Timothy had any sense, but I must confess I thought that you had. I was mistaken.'

Piers drew himself up and said, 'I went for the honour of the house. You would not like it to be said that this was the only house in the City that didn't send a prentice to help rescue Ned Buckle from the pillory.'

'Of course, you were not to know that Timothy would contrive to—er—mislay me in Thames Street, and answer the call as well,' said Uncle Gideon, and his voice was still very grave, but his mouth had begun to give little smiley twitches under his beard. 'I quite see that you felt the honour of the house rested on your shoulders.'

'Yes, sir,' said Piers, just as grave as Uncle Gideon.

'And so you rescued Ned Buckle. I think I saw him being carried past just now?'

'Oh yes, sir; and then the law students joined in, and a real mix-up started, and Timothy laid out a beadle—laid him out flat. Otherwise we'd have been home long ago.'

'Ah,' said Uncle Gideon. 'I imagine that was when you got that split lip.'

Piers smiled, slowly and rather carefully. It hurts to smile with a split lip. 'No, sir,' he said; 'that was on the way home. We met Toby Meredith with a few friends, and he said his father made better armour than you did. But I do really think I made a worse mess of his face than he has of mine.'

'Piers,' said his father, more solemnly than ever, 'I am grateful to you for your championship.' Then he looked from Piers to Timothy and back again, and said, 'You should both be thoroughly ashamed of yourselves, but obviously you are not ashamed of yourselves in the least. Perhaps we had better consider the matter closed.'

'*Thank* you, sir!' said Piers and Timothy at the same moment, and Giles, who had been staring at them in great admiration all this time, said suddenly, 'I say, Piers, I didn't think you could fight. I say, I'm sorry I said you couldn't hit anybody.'

At the same instant Beatrix cast herself down at Pier's feet and cried, 'My Heroic Brother!' in her best Catherine of Aragon manner.

'Get along with you,' said Piers, ungratefully.

But Beatrix didn't. She was enjoying herself. 'I *scorned* you,' she announced. 'I said it was *mortifying* to have a brother who stayed at home when the other prentices were out fighting the Watch, and Tamsyn said she'd hit me with her sugar pig if I said it again. And all the time you were being a hero!'

All at once Aunt Deborah, who had been standing quite still, just looking on, sat down in her big carved chair and laughed and laughed as though she never meant to leave off, while everybody watched her in a rather surprised sort of way. But she did stop at last, quite suddenly, and said, 'Oh, Piers, your poor face! I'll have to bathe it. Timothy, go and change that jerkin; you're not fit to be seen, and bring this one down to me and I'll mend it to-morrow. Then you shall both have some supper—though indeed you don't deserve it.'

So Timothy took himself off to change his jerkin, and Aunt Deborah was just going to shoo Piers down to the kitchen to have his face bathed, when Littlest appeared in the staircase doorway, looking such a nice compact little cherub in his white night-rail, with Lammy clutched to his chest, but a rather sorry little cherub all the same. He trundled forward into the room with his lower lip trembling a little, and his eyes still full of sleep.

'Mammy,' said Littlest to Aunt Deborah, reproachfully, as though he thought it was her fault. 'Littlest has had a bad dream.'

'Oh, my poor Littlest!' said Aunt Deborah, dropping on her knees and holding out her arms to him. 'Come to Mammy! There now, evening's quite all right, my precious, my honey. Mammy will take you back to bed.' And above Littlest's head she looked at Piers. 'You'd better go down and ask Meg for some warm water, my dear, and I'll come down to bathe your face as soon as I can. Don't let Meg touch it; she's so clumsy.'

'Don't worry about it, Mother,' said Piers, smiling even more carefully than before, because his lip was beginning to stiffen. I can quite well clean it up myself.'

'No, just ask for the water. I won't be long,' said Aunt Deborah over her shoulder, as she began to lead Littlest upstairs.

'I'll come and help you,' said Beatrix. 'I'll do *anything* for you, Piers.'

'Oh no, you won't,' said Piers, very firmly. And then he looked at Tamsyn. She had been standing quite still on the edge of the crowd all the time, with her eyes fixed on his bruised face, feeling so proud of him that it hurt like having something hard and bright in her inside, and hoping and *hoping* that he would notice her.

And when Piers looked at her, she took a deep breath and screwed up her courage, and said, 'Per-lease, *I* would like to come and help you bathe your face.'

'Would you?' said Piers. 'Come along, then.'

The Almost-Twins started to say that it wasn't fair, but Piers took no notice of them. He held out a hand to Tamsyn, and they went downstairs together. And Tamsyn was very happy.

4 *The Wise Woman*

Piers was just as quiet and just as annoyingly steady as ever
next day, and after a little while it was as though he had never
taken the largest mallet and gone forth to rescue Ned Buckle from
the Watch, except for a small scar on his lip that stayed even after
the cut was healed. Still, the Almost-Twins were never again quite
so scornful of him as they had been before.

The days got longer, and the world greener, and the streets of London grew very hot indeed. The little strip of garden between the Dolphin House and the river grew gayer and gayer, with Canterbury bells and pansies and sops-in-wine, so that Aunt Deborah said it had never been so gay before, and that it must be because Tamsyn had helped her grow the flowers.

Tamsyn and Beatrix went on doing lessons with Aunt Deborah in the mornings, and Littlest began to do lessons too, but only very little ones because of not being very old yet; and in the afternoons, most days they went shopping. All through June the herb market was a mass of gold, piled from end to end with dandelions which children picked in Chelsea Meadows and brought in to be sold to the City folk. When Aunt Deborah saw the herb market golden from end to end, she said, 'It's time to make dandelion wine again' (she made it every year). So next day she and Beatrix and Tamsyn and Littlest and Meg the Kitchen all set out carrying large plaited-rush baskets, because it takes a lot of dandelions to make dandelion wine; and they came back with the baskets piled high with golden flower-heads, so that although it was a grey day the street seemed full of sunshine as they passed.

On festivals and holidays and every Sunday afternoon, Uncle Gideon and Piers and Timothy took their bows and their quivers of grey goose-feathered arrows, and went off to the fields beyond Temple Bar to practise at the archery butts. You see, in those days England still depended in wartime on her archers, just as she did in the days of Crécy and Agincourt. Yew trees were still planted in churchyards so that there should always be plenty of good, red yew-wood for English long-bows, and each of the grey geese feeding on village greens all up and down the country had six of their moulted pinions taken every year to be used for flighting clothyard arrows. Every Englishman who was over twelve years of age and not too old or sick to bend a bow was supposed to practise at the butts on holidays and Sunday afternoons. Quite a lot of them didn't, of course, but quite a lot of them did.

So on holidays, and every Sunday when church was over and dinner was over, most of the men and boys of London, from the richest merchant who was not too old, to the poorest surgeon's apprentice who was just old enough, went pouring out of the City by all its eight gates, to practise at the butts in Moorfields or Spitalfields or in the meadows north of the Strand; and amongst them went Uncle Gideon and Piers and Timothy.

One of these archery practice days was Midsummer's Eve— St. John's Eve, some folks called it—and on this particular Midsummer's Eve, just as the Dolphin House family were sitting down to dinner, Aunt Deborah suddenly decided that as it was such a lovely day, she and the children would come too, that afternoon, to watch the archery. Everybody thought this was a lovely idea, including Giles, who had a half-holiday from school (people didn't work much or go to school much on St. John's Eve). And so when dinner was over—and it had been a particularly nice dinner, with pancakes and raisins to finish up with—Aunt Deborah packed a basket with little loaves and butter and some more raisins. Then she washed the pancake stickiness off Littlest's face, and poked and patted Beatrix and Tamsyn to make them neat and tidy, while the menfolk fetched their bows and quivers and buckled their bracers (a bracer was a sort of guard to protect your sleeve from the bowstring) on to their left forearms. And then they all set out.

Aunt Deborah walked first, with Uncle Gideon beside her carrying Littlest as well as his bow stave, because it was rather a long way for anyone whose legs were as short as Littlest's. Littlest had new scarlet hose on, and was cuddling his dear Lammy. Then came Beatrix and Tamsyn, carefully holding up the skirts of their sheeps-russet gowns to keep them out of the dust. Then came Giles with Bunch on a strong leash. In two years' time Giles would be carrying his bow and going out to shoot at the butts with the other men of the family, and this made him feel very superior as he swaggered along behind the girls. Piers and Timothy came last of all, carrying their bow staves and making sure that nobody got lost in the crowd. It was really quite a procession.

The Dolphin House doorway was garlanded with St. John's wort and foxgloves and green birch branches, in honour of Midsummer's Eve, and so was the doorway of nearly every house they passed, so that all the narrow streets seemed to have been especially decked out for Tamsyn and the others to go by. Of course Tamsyn knew that they were not, but it was nice to pretend they were; so she went on pretending.

The little party went out through Ludgate with a stream of other people who were going to shoot at the butts like Uncle Gideon, or watch their menfolk shooting, like Aunt Deborah and the children. The sun shone yellow as a dandelion in a sky of milky blue, and the cuckoos called from the distant woods where the King's Grace rode amaying in the spring and hunted the red deer in the autumn. The gardens were full of roses and the hayfields spangled with tall golden buttercups; and people had put on their gayest doublets and kirtles of green and saffron, pink and purple and azure, as though they wanted to be as brilliantly coloured as the summer's day. There were people sprinkled all over the meadows in ones and twos and little merry companies, all strolling along in the direction of the butts; and Uncle Gideon and his family strolled with them.

It was nice in the meadow where the straw targets had been set up. Aunt Deborah and the children found a sloping bank and settled themselves comfortably at the foot of it, while Uncle Gideon and

Piers and Timothy went off to join the archers who were stringing their bows and gossiping among themselves. There were quite a lot of other people sitting on the grass, and before long Littlest trundled off to play with a little boy with curly black hair who belonged to another family farther along the bank. It was a nice bank, covered with warm, springy turf and starred with eyebright and tiny yellow clover, and the Almost-Twins and Tamsyn scrambled up to sit on top of it, where they could look all round them; and the meadows were so flat that the top of the bank was like the top of a little hill. London Town was behind them, and far away in front, shimmering in the sunlight like a fairy city, was Westminster. The tall, fretted towers of the Abbey, and Whitehall Palace, where the King's Grace danced with the Lady Anne Boleyn in the evenings when the candles were lit in the Hall (when he was not at Greenwich, that is), and the warm, huddled roofs of ordinary houses, and the green gardens of the old Palace stretching to the river, all so tiny that by holding out her hand and shutting one eye Tamsyn could make it look as though she was holding the whole City in the palm of her hand.

Then the shooting began. Some of the targets were four hundred paces apart, and all the full-grown men shot at those, because everybody over twenty-four years old had to be able to speed an arrow that distance. But Piers and Timothy went to shoot at targets a little nearer together, because they were not grown up yet. The afternoon wore on; the arrows droned ceaselessly as they flew, a warm, drowsy sound; the archers crossed and recrossed the meadows as they shot, and went to pluck out their arrows, and turned to shoot back; and Tamsyn began to get very sleepy, sitting there in the sunshine. She shook herself every now and then, and sat with her eyes very wide open, especially when Piers was shooting. Piers was a good bowman; he laid his whole body to the bow, instead of only pulling with his arms in the foreign way, as Master Roger Whitcome's prentice did, and his loose was beautifully smooth, and his arrow nearly always hit the straw target quite near the peg in the middle. Tamsyn was very proud of him, so that it made her feel quite pink inside. Still, she went on feeling sleepy.

Then the mother of the little boy with the curly black hair came and sat beside Aunt Deborah and began to talk about making dandelion wine, while the two little boys and Bunch tumbled over and over each other at the foot of the bank, playing queer, complicated games of their own.

'I say, I've had enough of this,' said Giles suddenly. 'Let's go and do something interesting.'

'If you had your bow you could shoot an arrow in the air, and we could notice where it fell, and walk on and on in that direction until we found an adventure,' suggested Beatrix.

'Well, I haven't got my bow,' said Giles; and he thought for a bit. Then he said, 'I know, we'll go down there to the hedge and get a straight hazel twig and throw it in the air, and then we'll notice which way it points, and walk that way—just as though it *was* an arrow.'

Tamsyn pricked up her ears, and stopped feeling in the least sleepy. Oh, if only they would let her come too!

Giles thought deeply for a little while, in case he got a better idea, but as he did not, he said, 'Yes, that's what we'll do. Midsummer is a fairy time and hazel is a Fairy Wood, so it's bound to bring us an adventure. Come along, Tamsyn,' and he slid down the bank. Beatrix and Tamsyn slid after him, picked themselves up and shook down their full green skirts.

'Where are you off to, my poppets?' asked Aunt Deborah, breaking off the discussion about dandelion wine.

'For a walk, please,' they said.

'Very well,' said Aunt Deborah; 'but don't go too far, and don't do anything dreadful.'

'We won't,' they promised, and they set out for the hazel trees at the far side of the meadow, taking care not to go in the way of the archers. When they got there, Giles chose a nice, straight hazel twig and cut it into a little rod a few inches long, and sharpened one end, and peeled it so that it would show white on the grass.

'This is the most solemn moment,' he said. 'We are about to challenge the Fates to lead us to an adventure. I hope you realize that, you girls?'

They said they did; and Giles stepped back and cried, 'Fast!' as an archer does when he shoots an arrow, to warn people to get out of the way, and flung the twig up into the air as hard as ever he could. The peeled wood caught the sunlight, and they watched it shining silver as it turned over and over against the blue sky, soaring up and up; then it plunged down again, and landed in the grass between Beatrix and Tamsyn.

They looked anxiously to see what direction it pointed in.

'I say!' said Giles, in an excited voice. 'It's pointing straight towards that old windmill on the high ground.'

And it was. The windmill stood up against the sky nearly a mile away, with its brown sails spread out in a beckoning sort of way.

They walked on and on across the meadows, the Almost-Twins in front and Tamsyn bringing up the rear, heading straight for the distant windmill. Little streams wandered down from the uplands through the meadows on their way to join the Thames, and among the pollard willows on the bank of one of these they found a very fat toad. They stayed for some while staring at the toad, while the toad stared back at them, with his bulging, diamond-bright eyes, his knobbly sides panting in and out like a little pair of

44

bellows. But the adventure was waiting, and so, after a time, they turned back to the stream. It was much too wide to jump, and as far up or down stream as they could see there was no bridge or stepping-stones.

'We could go back to the Strand,' suggested Beatrix. 'The stream goes under the road there.'

'I know that, you zany,' said Giles. 'We aren't going all that way just to find a bridge.' And he sat down on the bank and began undoing the points that kept his brown hose up. Tamsyn plumped down beside him in an instant, and kicked off her shoes and pulled down her scarlet-clocked stockings; but Beatrix didn't like the idea at all, and she didn't begin to take her stockings off until the other two had finished. But she took them off at last, and bunched up her skirts; and they all slipped down into the stream, carrying their shoes and stockings in their hands.

'O-oh!' squealed Beatrix.

'Yow!' yelped Giles.

'Lovely!' crooned Tamsyn.

The water flowed cold and bright and shiversome round their legs, and the trout-speckled pebbles at the bottom shifted under their feet, and the white water-buttercups were all about them as they waded through and climbed out, laughing, on the farther bank. The Almost-Twins sat down and dried their feet on wisps of grass, and put on their shoes and stockings again; but Tamsyn was used to going barefoot among the little round hills of Devon, and she stood waggling her toes in the warm grass and watching the bright drops of water sparkling between them, while the others fastened their stockings; and when they all went on again, she continued carrying her shoes in her hand.

They were still walking straight towards the windmill, but they never got to it. Instead, they came out through a tangle of hazel and alder and rosebay-willow-herb and found themselves on the edge of an unexpected garden. It was a very little garden, but as full of flowers as ever it could be, and at the far side was a cottage with a reed-thatch roof that came down very low, as though it was wearing a brown velvet cap pulled well on to keep its ears warm. It had no chimney, only a hole in the roof through which a blue plume of woodsmoke rose straight into the air, like a jay's feather in the velvet cap. Two little windows peered out from under the eaves, and the door stood open in a welcoming sort of way. Tall, plumy poplars grew behind the cottage, and there were three reed-thatched bee-hives on a bench against the wall, and all the little garden was murmurous with bees.

Tamsyn's heart went out to the garden the moment she saw it; and she climbed on to the lowest bar of a little gate in the hyssop and sweetbrier hedge, and leaned over to get a nearer look.

Just at first the garden seemed to be full and spilling over with nothing but roses: little white musk roses, dark-red cinnamon roses, York-and-Lancaster roses blooming red and white together on the same bush, sweet-brier and pink-frilled eglantine. But when she looked more carefully Tamsyn saw that there were plenty of other flowers there too, growing under and through and among the roses—painted ladies and sops-in-wine, pansies and sweetwilliam and snap-dragon, larkspurs as deeply blue as the evening sky, and tall, white lilies of the Madonna. It was like a garden in a fairy-tale, and the Fairy Feel hung over it as strong as the scent of the roses.

'Oh, *do* come away!' whispered Beatrix. 'It might belong to a witch.'

'Course it doesn't,' said Giles scornfully. 'There's a witchen tree by the door, and no witch can abide a witchen tree; you know that.'

'You'm right there; 'tis only white magic that can be woven where the witchen tree is—white magic and healing spells,' said a soft voice close by, and the three children jumped as though they had been caught stealing apples. Round a mass of rose-bushes near the gate hobbled a little old woman with a trowel in one hand and a piece of sacking in the other. Her hair was hidden under a huge white coif, and her eyes in her withered brown face were blue as the larkspurs in her garden.

'Come your ways in, my dears,' she said. 'Come your ways in and welcome.'

And Tamsyn knew by the sing-song lilt of her voice that the old woman was from Devonshire. She slid down from the bar of the gate, and raised the latch in a great hurry, and they all trooped in, Giles remembering to doff his bonnet and the two girls making their best curtsies. 'Thank you very much,' they said politely.

The old woman stood watching them with a little smile that pucker-ed her face into a thousand fine wrinkles, while Giles closed the gate behind them. Then she asked, 'And what do 'e want wi' old Tiffany Simcock, my dears? Not a lost lover to be brought back, nor straying cattle to be found. No, no, nor yet the shingles to be healed with a girdle of rushes. Is it a wart, now? Have one of ye a wart for old Tiffany to charm away?'

'Then you *are* a witch—a white witch!' cried Beatrix, half-way between being very thrilled and a little scared.

'White witch or Wise Woman, 'tis all the same thing,' said the owner of the garden. 'Is it a wart, now, my pretty?'

'Well—no—you see——' began Beatrix.

But Giles said quickly, 'We did not come wanting anything, mistress; we didn't know there was a cottage or a garden or—or any-thing here. We came out to watch our father and our brother Piers at archery practice, and then we got tired of it, so we threw a hazel twig in the air, and followed the way it pointed when it came down, to look for an adventure—and here we are.'

'My days!' said the Wise Woman. 'You'm bold children to do such a thing on Midsummer's Eve, and with the Fairy Wood too. The Good People might have led 'ee over the edge of the world for an adventure, instead of bringing 'ee here to old Tiffany. You'm not likely to find adventure hereabouts, but if so be as bread and honey will do instead—hyssop honey, my dears, and there 'bain't none so sweet as hyssop honey in all the wide world—why, then, you're welcome to that.'

They said Yes please, it *would,* and Thank you very much, for they were beginning to be hungry.

So the Wise Woman smiled and turned to lead the way up the turf path to the cottage, with the three trooping behind her. But in the doorway she turned once more, and looked from Giles to Beatrix and back again. 'You'm brother and sister, I reckon?' she said.

'Yes, mistress,' said Giles.

The Wise Woman nodded. 'But the little one; the little one who comes barefoot through the grass, *she*'m not your sister?'

'No, she's our cousin,' Beatrix explained. 'She lived in Devon with our grandmother, but our grandmother died, and so she lives with us now.'

The Wise Woman put down her trowel on a stool beside the door and dropped the piece of sacking over it, and took Tamsyn's face between her old gnarled hands, tipping it gently upwards and gazing into her eyes. 'Ai-ee,' she crooned, as Tamsyn smiled suddenly. 'I knew, I knew! Us of the west always knows one another. The stars were dancing over Torridge when you were born, my pretty.'

Tamsyn nodded her head between the Wise Woman's hands. 'But it's a long time since I came away,' she said. 'Almost four months.'

''Tis more than that since *I* last watched the tall ships of Bideford sail over the Bar,' said the Wise Woman, more as though she was speaking to herself than to Tamsyn. 'My man was a sailor, and he brought me here-along when the world was young, before your mother was born. Ah, well, he'm dead these many and many years ago.'

Giles had begun to shift from foot to foot in a hungry sort of way, hoping that she had not forgotten about the bread and honey. But she had not, for she suddenly let go Tamsyn's face and turned to the darkness of her kitchen, calling back over her shoulder, 'Come your ways in, my dears, and mind the step.'

So they came in, minding the step, which was a steep downward one. The kitchen seemed very dim and cool after the hot sunshine outside, and at first they could not see much but the red glow of a low fire on the hearth, and a shaft of sunlight that filtered in through the horn panes of a tiny window and slanted down, full of dancing golden dustmotes, to the rush-strewn floor. But as their eyes grew used to the gloom they saw bright copper pans, and bundles of herbs and green cheeses in linen bags hanging from the rafters, and a rough table with its top scrubbed creamy-white, and rows and rows of shelves all round the walls crowded with exciting-looking jars and pots and bundles, almost like an apothecary's shop. There was a crimson clove carnation in a green pot on the window-sill, too, and a little grey cat who had come out from a dim corner, arching her back and purring, to curve herself round the Wise Woman's ankles as her mistress toddled about the kitchen, fetching crocks and platters and setting out her best on the scrubbed table.

'Now,' she said, in a little while, 'pull up thicky stools, my dears, and sit 'ee down. Here is brown bread and honey-in-the-comb, a handful of strawberries, and warm white goats' milk. Draw up to the table, and God bless the meal.'

So Giles and Beatrix and Tamsyn drew up their stools to the table, and ate thick slices of coarse brown bread and gold-dripping honeycomb and little sweet scarlet strawberries, washed down with warm milk in a brown earthenware pitcher which they shared among them, while the Wise Woman sat on her stool beside the fire and watched them kindly. And when they were as beautifully full as they could possibly be, she got up and said that she would show them her garden—her real garden, where she grew her herbs.

The Almost-Twins were not really very interested in gardens, but they were nicely brought up, and knew that you could not eat somebody's bread and honey and then not be interested in their garden if they wanted to show it to you. So they said politely that they would like to see Mistress Simcock's garden. But, as you know, Tamsyn loved gardens and growing things, and she said, '*Please*', and pushed her stool back very quickly, and hopped up, licking her sticky fingers with her little pink tongue.

Mistress Simcock led them out of doors again, and round the house, stopping to pass the time of day with a white nanny-goat who was tethered, with her kid beside her, in a little green place of her own, to another garden at the back, which they had not guessed was there at all. It was a small square plot with the tall poplar trees standing like sentinels beyond it, and from hedge to hedge it was full of the soft colours and mingled scents of the herbs that grew there. A tiny wind had sprung up, and the tops of the taller herbs were swaying gently, scattering their fragrance to the warm air; and there was a ceaseless humming of bees among the flowerheads and a flittering of jewelled butterfly-wings in the sunshine. The Fairy Feel lay strong over this garden, too—stronger than in the flower-patch beyond the cottage. Even now, in the bright dayshine, it was an enchanted place, and later, when the blue Midsummer dusk came down, it would be one of those places which are thresholds of Fairyland itself.

The Wise Woman began to move up and down the narrow, mazy paths between her herbs, with the little grey cat walking before her with tail erect, and the three children following behind. Sometimes she stopped to touch an especial favourite with a touch so gentle that not a basking butterfly on a leaf or a pollen-spangled bee in a flower-cup was disturbed by it. 'These are my children,' she said. 'My fine tall sons and pretty daughters.' And she went on again, speaking the name of each plant as she came to it—names that sang themselves in Tamsyn's head like a magic charm.

'Borage, marjoram, foxgloves, wormwood, melilot, rose-of-the-sun,' crooned the Wise Woman. 'Bee-balm, bergamot, elacampane. Here's camomile; see her flowers like a thousand bright eyes smiling from the ground; and here are marigolds—brew the petals to drink when you have a cold. Cummin for sore eyes; rosemary and rue—I always grow them together, sweet and bitter, side by side. This is applemint, and this herb patience, and this sweet cicely from a convent garden; and southernwood, and tancies to flavour little cakes at Easter time. Here are my dandelions, and they would seed themselves all over my garden if I did not stop them, the bold creatures; priest's crown, some folks call them—ai-ee! but not the priest of these days, *they* wear no crowns, no, no; 'tis the priests of olden times, the priest-kings, the Druids, who gave the flower its name. They were wise men, the Druids; they knew the use of herbs and the white secrets of healing magic, but they weren't no wiser than old Tiffany Simcock, my days, no!'

Presently she stopped beside a flower like a giant harebell, and stooped to touch one of the flowerheads that drooped on the thread-slender stem. 'Rampion,' she crooned, 'that belongs to Themselves, the Pharisees, the Lordly People. You may set the bells a-ringing, but don't 'ee go for to pick the flower at Midsummer. 'Tisn't safe to meddle with aught that belongs to Themselves, at Midsummer; not with elder-blossom, nor yet white foxgloves, nor yet with rampion.' And she turned to the children behind her. 'Do 'ee remember that, my dears.'

'We will,' they said.

And Tamsyn said, 'Please, have you any white foxgloves in this garden?'

'Aye, down beside the poplar trees. I grow all the fairy flowers. I grow them to please the Fairy People who come to me. All gardens have a few Pharisees, all gardens and all places, but my garden has very many. They come and go like the winds, but there is never a time when my garden is quite without its Pharisees.' And she turned her head as though to watch something fluttering among the leaves of a yellow-flowered mullion; while the little grey cat raised its head and watched, too, with wide amber eyes.

'Please,' asked Tamsyn, 'can you see Them?' She hoped it was not rude to ask; she did so want to know.

'Ai-ee, I can see Them,' replied the Wise Woman. 'I was born on Midsummer's Eve, and so was my mother before me, and the first thing I ever mind seeing was the Proud People hovering against the moon, and their eyes like sparks, and their wings pearled by the moonshine. Them as flies in the sunshine, and them as comes with the moon, and them as flitters in the twilight betwixt and between; old Tiffany knows them all, and they knows old Tiffany.'

And she toddled on again, stopping to touch a flower here and a leaf there as she passed, until they had gone right round the garden and got back to the cottage. Then Beatrix said in her most grown-up way, 'I think we ought to be going, Mistress Simcock. It must be quite late.'

'And your mother will be wondering what has come to 'ee,' nodded the Wise Woman. 'But first you shall each have a gift to take back with 'ee, for 'tis not often as folks comes to old Tiffany without they has the shingles to be struck for, or warts to be charmed away.'

'Oh, but we don't want you to give us anything,' began Beatrix primly. 'Thank you very much for the bread and honey, but——'

Giles kicked her. He saw no sense in refusing a present when one came your way; and anyhow, the Wise Woman had already gone indoors, leaving them in the sunshine before the cottage. In a little while she came back carrying the promised gifts. ''Tis little enough, perhaps,' she said, 'but 'twill be something to remember old Tiffany by.' There was a blue earthenware pot of run-honey for Giles, a necklace of carved cherry stones strung on a scarlet thread for Beatrix; and for Tamsyn there were her shoes and stockings which she had forgotten, and a brown bulb something like an onion.

'For the little one with the bare feet,' said the Wise Woman, 'because you have the fairy's gift of green fingers, even if you can't see the Fairy People. Plant it in a pot and keep it in the dark until it shoots, and then put it in a warm window. Tend it well, and love it dearly as all growing thing need to be loved, and it will flower at Christmas time and bring you your heart's desire.'

Tamsyn looked at her a little doubtfully. When she first came to London her heart's desire had been simply to go home again at once, to her own dear Devon, and her other heart's desire had always been to be a boy, so that she could sail with one of those tall ships of Bideford, that were for ever outward bound over the Bar or homing up-river from half the world away. But now it had spread, and got mixed up with Piers and the *Dolphin and Joyous Venture,* which was all rather muddling; and of course the Wise Woman could not be expected to know that, and she could not explain about it—not with the Almost-Twins there, too. But the Wise Woman was very wise, even among other wise women, and perhaps she did know after all; she took Tamsyn's face between her hands once more, and bent to look at her, long and closely, with those wonderful larkspur-blue eyes.

'I shall never go home,' she said at last. 'I stay here with my garden, my fine sons and pretty daughters; but you will go home, one day—one day—and then you shall have your heart's desire, *all* your heart's desire. And when you go home, little maid, remember me, and call my name to the West Wind and the surf along the Pebble Ridge, and give my love to the Torridge as it flows under Bideford Bridge, and to the steep combes and the mewing buzzards, so that they shall remember me, too.'

And Tamsyn said, 'I will! Oh, I *will!*'

The Wise Woman stooped, and dropped a kiss on the top of her head. 'Now you must go,' she said, 'all of you. Run—run, my chickens, or your mother will be thinking you're lost.'

So they thanked her again, politely, and went scurrying down the path to the gate. They looked back once, after closing it behind them, and saw her still standing in the doorway of the fairy-seeming cottage, with the little grey cat sitting beside her. She waved to them, and they waved back; then they plunged into the tangle of elder and hazel that shut the enchanted garden away from the workaday world.

The sun was getting low, though it would not set for a long while yet, and the shadows of tree and cottage and hedgerow lay far across the golden meadows, and the larks had dropped out of the sky. But the cuckoos were still calling from the distant woods.

'I wonder if she's mad,' said Giles. 'It was rather a nice sort of mad, if she was.' And he opened the pot of honey and stuck in one finger.

'Of course she wasn't,' said Beatrix, putting on her cherry-stone necklace. 'Wise Women always say queer things; it comes of being so wise.'

But Tamsyn didn't say anything—not anything at all. There was a lovely warm feeling of happiness inside her that seemed to sing very softly; and she nursed the fat brown bulb which was to flower at Christmas and bring her her heart's desire, and thought long thoughts all by herself, a little behind the other two.

They had just put on their shoes and stockings again after crossing the stream—Tamsyn, too, this time—when they met Piers and Timothy.

'Well, you *are* a bright party,' said Piers. 'We thought you'd been carried off by Barbary Pirates at the very least, and Mother sent us to look for you because it's time to go home—more than time.'

'I say, we're very sorry,' said Giles, and began to explain about the search for adventure, and the Wise Woman, and how it got rather later than they thought; but Piers said, 'Never mind about that now; the thing to do is to get back.'

And Timothy squinted like a bull-frog at everybody in turn, and said cheerfully, 'My eye! *You'll* catch it, I shouldn't wonder.'

'One day when you do that,' said Giles, rising in his wrath, 'you'll stick like it, an' you'll have to be led round the country from fair to fair with a collar round your neck like a dancing bear, an' some people will pay to see you, but *I* shan't.'

'Stop it, both of you,' said Piers, in a voice that sounded surprisingly like the one Uncle Gideon used when he meant to be instantly obeyed. Neither Giles nor Timothy had ever heard him speak like that before, and they were so astonished that they actually stopped. Then he took Tamsyn's hand in a comforting sort of way, and said in a quite different voice, 'Don't you worry, Tamsy.'

'I'm not,' said Tamsyn stoutly. 'And I'm *used* to being spanked.' Nothing, not even a spanking, could spoil the warm singing-gladness inside her, or take the magic out of Midsummer's Eve.

But there was no smacking for anyone, after all.

When they got back to the place where they had started from, they found that almost everybody had gone home to supper, and Aunt Deborah was sitting with Littlest half asleep on her lap and Uncle Gideon pacing up and down close by and looking rather grim. The moment she saw them she dumped Littlest on the grass and jumped up and came to meet them.

'Where did you find them?' she demanded. 'Oh, deary me, you really are naughty poppets. It's past Littlest's bedtime and we shall be so late for supper. You don't *deserve* any supper, and you must be so hungry.'

So Giles began to explain, and Bunch came barking round them, and Uncle Gideon came stalking up, still looking very grim, but with his eyebrows cocked up inquiringly.

'It was my fault,' said Giles, standing with his feet apart and his hands behind his back (but still carrying the pot of honey). 'I got tired of watching the archery, and so I threw a stick up in the air, and we walked the way it pointed when it came down, to look for an adventure.'

'Ah,' said Uncle Gideon. 'And by the time you have been away, I gather that you found one?'

'Well, not exactly, sir,' said Giles. 'We found a Wise Woman, and she said she came from Devon, and she gave us bread and honey, and then she showed us her garden and it got later than we knew—well, I mean to say we couldn't eat her bread and honey and then not look at her garden when she wanted to show it to us, could we, sir?'

'I see your point,' said Uncle Gideon.

'And *that's* why we were late, because we *couldn't* eat her bread and honey and then not be interested in her garden,' said Giles virtuously. 'I mean you *can't* go round eating people's bread and honey, and then——'

'Giles,' said Uncle Gideon, 'if you mention bread or honey again, I shall be seriously displeased.'

'Sorry, Father.'

'And may I ask what is in that pot you are so carefully hiding behind your back?'

Giles turned bright pink, and swallowed hard. 'Honey,' he said.

Uncle Gideon covered his eyes with his hand and said, 'I cannot bear it!' And pretty Aunt Deborah began to laugh. She tried not to, but she couldn't help it; so they knew that everything was going to be all right, and there would be no spanking.

Beatrix explained, 'The Wise Woman gave it to him, and she gave me this necklace, and she gave Tamsyn a thing to grow in a pot.'

And Tamsyn held out the precious bulb, gazing beseechingly at Aunt Deborah. 'Look!' she said eagerly. 'She said I was to put it in a pot in a warm window and it will flower at Christmas, and *please,* Aunt Deborah, can I have a pot?'

Aunt Deborah took the bulb and looked at it. 'I believe it's a tulip,' she said, quite forgetting, for the moment, about being late for Littlest's bedtime, because she never *could* resist bulbs of any sort, and tulips were very rare and precious things in those days. Even the King's Grace had very few of them in his gardens at Westminster, growing with other strange and rare things, such as white lilac and winter jasmine and passion flowers. As Tamsyn had never seen one she asked, 'Please, what is a tulip?'

'Wait until it flowers, and see for yourself,' said Aunt Deborah, giving the precious bulb carefully back into Tamsyn's hands. 'But I don't think it will flower before the spring, however warm you keep it.' Then she remembered about it being late, and said, 'And now we really must go home, or we shall never get any supper at all.'

So they collected Littlest and set out for home.

London still seemed a long way off, and not quite real, with all its crowding towers and spires and pointed gables tinted lilac and tawny by the evening light; and suddenly, as the sun sank lower, it began to flash back from the glass-filled windows of churches and rich folks' houses, so that the City was a city in a dream, a city of golden windows.

Piers and Tamsyn were walking behind the others, hand in hand; and 'Look!' said Tamsyn, 'London has golden windows.'

'So it has, Tamsy,' said Piers, and that was all, but Tamsyn knew that he liked the golden windows as much as she did. That was one of the very nice things about being with Piers—you always knew he understood.

As they got nearer, the golden windows faded, but when they passed through Ludgate, the City was full of Midsummer magic, all the same, and the crowds in the streets were one and all just a little fairy-kissed, so that if a white cat in a golden kirtle, or an enchanted prince, or a pumpkin travelling-wagon drawn by harvest mice, were suddenly to appear among them, Tamsyn would not have been in the least surprised. The streets were mostly in blue shadows now, but if you looked upward the steep roofs were still warm in the sunshine—pointed, leaning roofs of russet and tawny and coral-pink, where the pigeons fluttered and perched, crooning in the evening warmth, and here and there was still a golden window, after all. The green birch branches that shaded every door, and the foxgloves and orpin and white Madonna lilies, were all beginning to cast long, fairy-seeming shadows; and every house had its lamps before the door, green and yellow, crimson and rose-pink, waiting to be lit when the twilight came.

Some of the Midsummer magic got into Tamsyn's toes, and took the tiredness out of them, so that she gave a little hop every three steps. And a little more of the Midsummer magic had found its way into the tulip bulb—or perhaps the Wise Woman had put it there before she gave the bulb to Tamsyn, to make sure that it *would* flower at Christmas and bring her her heart's desire, in spite of what Aunt Deborah said about tulips not flowering before the spring. It felt warm and alive in her hand, as though the flower inside it was stirring in its sleep; and she nursed it close against her as she pattered along beside Piers, with that little hop every three steps, because of the magic in her toes.

Piers said, 'Was it a tremendously good adventure, Tamsy?'

And Tamsyn gave an extra hop, and said, 'It was loverly! But I do wish you could have had it too.'

And that same moment they reached the Dolphin House; and the carved and painted dolphins seemed even more joyfully adventurous than usual, as they stared down with their little rolling eyes, through the green branches and fairy-foxgloves and St. John's wort, at Piers and Tamsyn standing below—as though the Midsummer magic that had got into Tamsyn's toes and the tulip bulb had got into them too. And perhaps it had. Queer things happen at Midsummer.

5 *How Tamsy Saw the Laughing Lady*

The next day Aunt Deborah gave Tamsyn a green earthenware pot, and Tamsyn filled it with earth from the garden, which she picked over carefully for stones or sharp things that might scratch or worry a baby tulip, and planted the precious bulb in it, and put it in a dark cupboard in the still-room. After that she visited it two or three times every day, to make sure that it was all right and see if it could have begun to shoot since the last time she came.

Summer drew on, and in the open country Tamsyn knew that the hay harvest would be all over and the wheatfields turning from green to gold, and in the hedges there would be meadow-sweet and little wild convolvulus striped pink and white, like marchpane. In the garden behind the Dolphin House the lavender was in flower, and Aunt Deborah picked it with Tamsyn's help, and laid it out on the turf-plot to dry in the sun before she made it into packets to go among her linen in the big linen-press in the still-room and mixed it with the strewing herbs. And the gooseberries on the three gooseberry bushes that shared the bottom of the garden with the quince tree were swelling out. Soon they would be big and bursty-soft, and sweet to taste and golden to look at; and when you held one up to the sunlight you would be able to see the shadows of the seeds inside it.

All the family were waiting for those gooseberries to ripen. But Littlest didn't want to wait until then. He liked gooseberries to be hard and green and eye-watering sharp. Even when they gave him a pain he still liked them like that. Nothing that anybody could say or do would keep Littlest from going straight back to those gooseberry bushes the moment they took their eye off him—and quite soon there would be no gooseberries left!

'Peacocks love gooseberries,' Beatrix and Giles told him over and over again. 'If you go on eating green gooseberries, you know what will happen to you. You'll turn into a peacock, and probably you'll be eaten at the Lord Mayor's Banquet, because the Lord

Mayor is very fond of roast peacock.'

Littlest looked a bit worried when they told him this, but he went on eating green gooseberries all the same. And then one day the dreadful thing happened!

Aunt Deborah had gone to spend the afternoon with Mistress Whitcome two doors down the street to help her cut out a new kirtle from a length of orange damask that Master Whitcome had given her for a birthday present; Meg the Kitchen was scouring pans with a great clattering and scraping, and the children were left to themselves in the garden. Tamsyn had just been into the kitchen to borrow a slice of saffron cake from Meg, and it had taken her a little while to do it, because Meg was rather deaf and was making such a tremendous clattering with the pots and pans. When she came out into the garden again she saw something so astonishing and frightful that she could only stand quite still and gasp. She even dropped the piece of cake. The Almost-Twins were sitting side by side on the still-room windowsill, gazing vaguely up into the sky and doing nothing in particular; and up the path from the gooseberry bushes came Littlest, strutting along and pulling Lammy behind him on the end of a piece of cord. And Littlest had grown a peacock's tail!

He looked quite all right otherwise; in fact he looked very nice, with his red-gold hair and his bright-blue eyes and his scarlet stockings. But there, growing out from under the skirts of his doublet and trailing behind him along the path, were five long peacock feathers gleaming green and gold and blue in the sunlight. Poor Littlest had eaten green gooseberries once too often!

The Almost-Twins seemed to notice what had happened practically at the same moment as Tamsyn did, and blank horror spread over their faces. Then Giles got up and went to Littlest, saying sorrowfully, 'Oh, Littlest, we *did* warn you— and it's happened.'

Littlest stood with his legs wide apart, and looked up at Giles a little puzzled, with a bit of green gooseberry skin stuck to his chin.

'You must be very brave,' said Giles, 'Look what's growing out of you behind.'

Littlest screwed round and looked behind him over his shoulder, and saw the peacock's tail spreading out across the path with all its jewelled eyes bright in the sunshine. For a long, breathless moment he simply stared, and then he opened his mouth and let out an agonized yell. 'Pully out!' yelled poor Littlest. 'Pully out! Pully out!'

Beatrix flung herself down beside him, and raised imploring arms to Giles. 'Oh, do not tell the Lord Mayor,' she cried. 'Peacocks are so very scarce this year.'

'I think we ought to tell him,' said Giles. 'He's bound to find out, anyway.'

'Oh no, not if we hide Littlest very carefully,' cried Beatrix, wringing her hands. 'We can hide him in Kit's Castle and feed him on corn and branmash. Nobody must know that he has turned into a peacock.' And she flung her arms round Littlest, who promptly hit her on the head with Lammy and went on roaring, 'Pully out! Pully out!'

Never mind, Littlest darling,' cried Beatrix distractedly. 'We love you just the same, even if you *are* a peacock.'

'Poor Mother!' said Giles gloomily, taking no notice of Littlest's yells. 'She'll never believe, when we take her up to Kit's Castle and show her a peacock, that it's really Littlest.'

But Beatrix said, 'Of *course* she will. Mothers always know their own children, even when they've grown feathers.' And she clasped Littlest more closely to her, while he roared louder than ever.

And at that moment two things happened: the back door opened and Piers came out into the garden and shut it behind him; and Tamsyn saw that the peacock's feathers were fastened on to the skirts of Littlest's doublet with a large pin. They were the five feathers from the play-chest in Kit's Castle!

Piers demanded, 'What are you doing to Littlest?' And then he saw the peacock's tail and Tamsyn frozen rigid with astonishment, and the Almost-Twins wringing their hands and shouting that Littlest was turning into a peacock. He did not waste an instant. He went straight across to Littlest and pushed Beatrix firmly out of the way and squatted down and put an arm round the terrified little boy.

'Pully out! Oh, *do* pully out!' wept Littlest.

'Of course I'll pull it out,' said Piers consolingly. 'You hold tight to Tamsy, and I'll pull it out this moment.'

So Tamsyn came unfrozen and flew to sit on her heels in front of Littlest, and hold him tight round the middle, and Littlest clung to her, sobbing and hiccoughing and rubbing his teary face against her, so that she thought she had never noticed properly before what a dear little boy Littlest was; and Piers took a firm hold of the peacock's tail. 'Now,' he said, 'hold tight.' And he pulled, and he pulled, and he pulled, while the Almost-Twins stood by and offered helpful advice, and Bunch looked on in an interested sort of way.

'Pully out!' bellowed Littlest. 'Pully *out!*'

'He's pulling it out, darlin',' crooned Tamsyn. 'Almost out, darlin'; hold tight to Tamsy.'

'Ugh!' grunted Piers, pulling harder than ever with one hand and slipping out the pin with the other. 'It's coming. It's— almost—out—now. One more—pull—and it's—OUT.' And the tail *was* out, and Piers fell over backwards into a lavender bush.

Everybody sorted themselves out and picked themselves up and looked at each other, Littlest hiccoughing and rubbing his seat, and Piers holding the five long peacock's feathers in his hand.

'There,' said Piers. 'That's all over. But I shouldn't go eating any more green gooseberries, if I were you, or it might happen again.'

Littlest shook his head and rubbed harder than ever. His chest was still heaving with sobs, but he swallowed them manfully, and promised, 'Littlest *won't!*'

'Anyway, you have some peacock feathers of your own now,' said Piers.

Littlest's sobs and hiccoughs broke off between one sob and the next hiccough. He stopped rubbing his seat, and a slow smile spread over his teary face, and he put out his hands for the lovely jewel-bright feathers that were so exactly like the ones in the play-chest, which he had never been allowed to touch. 'For Littlest?' he said, rather uncertainly, because it seemed too good to be true.

'Of course,' said Piers. 'You grew them, didn't you?' and gave him the feathers.

'Yes, but——' said the Almost-Twins with one voice, looking very blank.

Piers turned on them, with his eyebrows cocked up towards his red hair. 'There's no "but" about it,' he said. 'Littlest grew these feathers himself, and of course they are his to keep.'

'Yes, but——' began Giles again.

Piers looked at him very hard, and asked politely, 'You were going to say?'

And Giles turned very red and swallowed and didn't say any more.

And Beatrix said, 'Oh, I see,' in a very small voice.

Littlest, with the tears still wet on his cheeks and his face wreathed in smiles, was gazing lovingly at his precious feathers. Tamsyn gazed at Piers with her mouth and eyes very wide open in admiration, and then suddenly she saw how funny it all was, and she collapsed on to the grass and sat there with her russet skirts flung out round her, kicking her heels and laughing, laughing, laughing. For a moment everybody just looked at her inquiringly, and then Piers began to laugh, too, and even the Almost-Twins joined in, and Bunch sat down with his tongue lolling out of his mouth, as though he were laughing most of all. But Littlest just went on smiling lovingly at his peacock's feathers.

When they had all laughed until they felt quite weak and silly, they just sat round on the little grass plot and looked at each other, while they got their breath back. It seemed very quiet in the garden, after all the noise and excitement of the last few minutes—a hot, sleepy sort of quietness made up of lots of small sounds: the scraping and clattering of Meg still scouring pans in the kitchen, the distant song of a Jenny-whitethroat in somebody else's garden, the droning of brown velvet bees among the sweet-william and snapdragon and peonies, the murmur of the City, the whisper of the Thames below the garden wall. Tamsyn wriggled over to the piece of saffron cake which was lying under the lavender bush where she had dropped it when all the excitement began, and gathered it up carefully; it had been slightly sat on and squashed well into the dark earth of the flower-bed, but when she had dusted the pieces it was almost as good as new.

It was nice sitting on the warm grass in the sunshine and eating saffron cake.

'I say, did Meg give you that?' asked Giles, hopefully.

Tamsyn nodded, with her mouth full.

'Then she must be in a very good temper,' said Giles. 'I think I'll just go and see——' And he scrambled to his feet without even waiting to finish what he was saying.

'You'll have to shout awful loud, to make her hear above the pots and pans,' Tamsyn called after him.

Piers uncurled his long legs too; he ought to be at work, of course. He was supposed to be blowing up the forge fire for old Caleb, who was working on a breastplate of white steel which had been ordered by My Lord Guildford. He had come out when he heard Littlest's shrieks, but now he must go back again, although he didn't much want to. Then he stopped quite still in a half-getting-up position, with his head turned towards the river, listening; and Giles, who had got as far as the house door, stopped and listened too. A faint noise of shouting and a lilt of music stole into the hot stillness of the garden from somewhere far down river, a long, long way off, but coming nearer every moment.

'Please, what is it?' asked Tamsyn.

'I say, something's coming up the river,' said Giles.

'It must be a Great Noble,' cried Beatrix. 'There are musicians —and listen to people shouting! Oh, Piers, you don't suppose it's the King's Grace, do you?'

Piers said, 'I wonder. It might be him coming up from Greenwich to Westminster. Come on, let's go and look,' and he sprang to his feet and went swinging down the garden.

Tamsyn kilted up her skirts and flew after him, and Bunch and the Almost-Twins brought up the rear; but Littlest still sat where he was, smiling peacefully at the five peacock's feathers that seemed to stare back at him with all their round, jewelled eyes.

The barges and tilt-boats on the river were all drawing in to shore, leaving the way clear for whatever it was that was coming upstream. The thread of music was growing louder and shriller and sweeter every moment, and they could hear words in the shouting now, 'God save your Grace!' The people were shouting, 'Harry! God save King Hal!'

'It *is* the King's Grace,' shouted Giles. 'The King's Grace coming up from Greenwich.'

'Help me up, please. Help-me-up-quick-this-minute,' gabbled Tamsyn, bunching her skirts higher still, and beginning to scramble on to the turf seat against the wall.

Piers swung her up and set her on her feet. 'Don't fall in the river,' he said, and dumped Beatrix beside her, and Giles scrambled up on his own.

The noise and shouting and the music were much closer now, and Tamsyn was so excited that she almost forgot to breathe. The flash and flicker of the river seemed to grow suddenly brighter, as though the hurrying ripples were excited too, because they were carrying the King's Grace through his City, between banks crowded with people who loved him, to his great palace of White-hall.

'Why does the King's Grace live all the time at Greenwich, when he has such a lovely palace at Westminster?' shouted Tamsyn, above the noise of cheering.

'Because it's half-way between Deptford and Woolwich,' Piers told her. 'The King's ships are built there, in the Royal Dockyards, and he likes watching them being built.'

Then the noise and cheering suddenly swelled into a roar, and Piers shouted over his shoulder, 'Littlest! Hi! It's the King's Grace! Run!'

Littlest came out of his dream with a jump, and he bundled to his feet and came rushing down the garden, waving the peacock's feathers above his head and shouting joyfully, 'Littlest see the King's Grace! Littlest see the King's Grace!' and Piers caught him and swung him up to his shoulder, just as a great barge full of musicians came into sight. It was rowed by eight watermen, and painted crimson and emerald-green and gilded with bright gold leaf that was as yellow as marsh-marigolds; and the musicians in it were playing flutes and recorders and lutes and rebecks, and two in the bows were blowing long trumpets that had square banners hanging from them, blue as the night sky and worked all over with golden Tudor roses. Oh, the musicians' barge was lovely, but it was nothing compared with the Royal Barge that came behind it.

A great barge with high gilded prow, and bulwarks hung with tapestries as softly coloured as a pigeon's breast. Twelve rowers bent to the gilded oars, all dressed in liveries of white and green, for those were the Tudor colours, and all with golden roses embroidered on their breasts and backs; and in the stern, under a canopy of crimson brocade, lounged the fat, jolly figure of the King's Grace, with the Queen beside him.

People were hanging out of windows and swarming along wharves and down river stairs, to shout for bluff King Hal, God bless him!

And the six crowded together on the turf seat at the bottom of the Dolphin House garden cheered and shouted with the rest, all except Bunch, who barked instead; but Tamsyn noticed that none of them, not one person in all the crowds that thronged the water-side, seemed to be shouting for the Queen.

The barge was almost opposite the foot of the garden now, and quite close inshore, and Tamsyn could see both the King's Grace and the Queen quite well. King Hal looked jolly and kind, and he was laughing, with his plump face crinkled up into merry lines under his jewelled bonnet, while he beat time with one fat hand glistening with rings to the tune the minstrels were playing. But Tamsyn was not sure that she liked the King's Grace, although she knew that he was a very good King and that his people loved him and she ought to love him too, because he was building a Navy for England and making England great among the nations of the world. So she looked at the Queen instead. People still called the Queen just Ann Boleyn, or 'The Lady', because they didn't like her. But Tamsyn liked her. Tamsyn thought that she was lovely in just the same way as the music floating back over the bright water from the musicians' barge was lovely. She was not pretty, exactly, but she had a laughing face, and her head was set on her long, slim neck as a flower is set on its stem. She was wearing the Royal colours: a gown of white over a kirtle of softest green—just the green of young beech leaves when they first uncurl in the spring and the sun shines through them—and her great, filmy, bell-shaped sleeves were green, too, and all webbed over with gold. Her black hair was gathered into a jewelled net in the newest French fashion, and there were milky pearls in her ears and about her long throat, and her skin seemed to Tamsyn to be as white as the pearls, so that the only things about her that were not white or gold or green were her red, red mouth and her black, black eyes. And her mouth was laughing, but her eyes were terribly unhappy behind the laughter.

Tamsyn wondered if she was unhappy because the people were not shouting for her at all, but only for the King's Grace; and Tamsyn thought it was horrid of them. At that moment Anne Boleyn looked up and saw the six of them crowded on the turf seat, Beatrix and Giles and Tamsyn, and Bunch wagging his tail and barking, and Littlest sitting on Piers' shoulder and flourishing his bright peacock's feathers above his head. And Tamsyn took a deep breath, and shouted as loud as ever she knew how, 'God save the Queen!' The Queen should have one person to shout for her, anyway!

And next instant Piers took up the cry, his voice cracking in the middle because it had not finished breaking yet, 'God save the Queen!'

So the Queen had two people to shout for her after all.

She must have heard them, because for a moment she looked up straight at Tamsyn, and though she was laughing still, her laughter was quite different— warm and gentle and sweet, so that Tamsyn thought what a lovely Mammy she must be for the little year-old Princess Elizabeth to have.

Then the Royal Barge had swept by, and the joyous lilting music was growing fainter and fainter, and other barges were following in its wake, not so fine as the Royal one, to be sure, but very gay all the same, bringing the Lords and Ladies of the Court back to Westminster.

'I say, didn't the King's Grace look jolly,' said Giles, jumping down from the turf seat.

'*I* liked the Queen best,' said Tamsyn, very softly, still looking after the gay barges that were shrinking to be as small as water-beetles in the distance, and listening to the last faint whisper of the lovely music.

Beatrix tossed her red hair back over her shoulders, and said in a pleased sort of voice, 'People say she's a wicked woman.'

'They only say that because they loved Queen Catherine, and the Lady took her place,' said Piers, setting Littlest on his own short legs once more. 'And that is not her fault. The King's Grace got tired of Queen Catherine and wanted Queen Anne instead— and he always has what he wants, no matter who gets hurt by it.'

Giles said, 'If you go round saying things like that, you'll get your head cut off one day, I shouldn't wonder. And anyway, I shouldn't have thought *you'd* find any fault with the King's Grace, and him building three ships at a time in Deptford.'

But Piers only said quietly, 'I'm going back to work now, or I shall get a hiding.' And he went.

Tamsyn never forgot seeing the Queen go by from Greenwich to Westminster. In after years, when the King's Grace had got tired of Anne too, and she had gone, laughing still, with her proud head very high, to her death on Tower Green, and people said more than ever that she had been a wicked woman, Tamsyn remembered her always as she had seen her that summer's day, in her white gown with the winged green sleeves, looking up at her with lovely, kind laughter, before the barge swept her on and away. She always remembered, too, the desperate unhappiness in the Queen's eyes. And she never believed a single word against the Laughing Lady.

6 *Tall Ship Magic*

One day in September Aunt Deborah and the children had an
an invitation to spend the afternoon with Mistress Whitcome, and
they all went, except Tamsyn. Tamsyn had a really dreadful cold.
She had had it for days, and Aunt Deborah had given her red-pepper
lozenges and doses of honey-and-vinegar, which was so horrid
that she would rather have had the cold, but she was still sneezy
and coldy and slightly cross when the day of the invitation came,
and as it was a grey, raw, drizzly afternoon, Aunt Deborah said
she must stay at home.

'We shall be back by Littlest's bedtime,' said Aunt Deborah.
'Meg will give you your afternoon bread and raisins, and you
may go up and play in the attic if you like, but you are not to go
into the garden, because if you do your cold will fly straight to
your chest, and then I shall put you to bed with a fennel poultice on
it—the chest, I mean, not the cold, though of course it comes to the
same thing really—and you will not like that at all.'

And she gave Tamsyn another red-pepper lozenge, with a dried
apricot for afterwards to take the taste away, and several of Uncle
Gideon's largest kerchiefs, and went away with Littlest and the
Almost-Twins.

Tamsyn watched them go from the parlour window, Aunt
Deborah in her best blue damask gown and Beatrix in her best leaf-
green, Giles with his red hair newly brushed until it shone, and
Littlest with Lammy in his hand and a jaunty feather in his cap,
all looking very festive. Tamsyn did not particularly want to spend
the afternoon with Mistress Whitcome, who was stout and stately,
and a bit dull, though kind; but it was lonely after they had gone,
and her face ached and her nose was sore and her head felt stuffy, and
altogether she was miserable and forlorn and coldy. Besides, she had
a loose tooth, the sort that gets pushed up by the one underneath,
so that it wobbles about and hurts, without being loose enough to
come out. Of course the sensible thing would have been to tell
Uncle Gideon about it, so that he could pull it out; but Uncle

Gideon was one of those people who pull out teeth scientifically, with loops of thread round them. People who do it like that always say that it is the best way; but Tamsyn had seen him pulling out one of Beatrix's teeth only a few weeks ago, and she didn't want it to happen to *her*. So she hadn't mentioned her tooth to anybody, in case Uncle Gideon should get to hear about it. She poked at it hopefully every now and then, to see if it had got any looser since the last poke, but it never had, and it hurt worse when she poked it. Even Bunch had deserted her and gone to spend the afternoon with Meg the Kitchen. Everything was perfectly horrid.

Tamsyn took out the red-pepper lozenge which she had been sucking and glared at it. Then she dropped it into the back of the hearth, and ate the dried apricot, to see if that would make her feel more cheerful, but it didn't much. So she drifted across to the window again, and looked at her precious tulip. She had brought it out of the dark cupboard nearly a week ago, and put it there, because it had begun to shoot, just as the Wise Woman had said it would. There was a thick, pale-green snout sticking up through the brown soil, and Tamsyn touched it very gently with the tip of one finger, wondering what it would be like when it flowered at Christmas: cup-shaped or star-shaped or bell-shaped? Blue or yellow or crimson? That did cheer her up a bit, just for the moment, because it was a very satisfying little green snout, and she loved it dearly.

She sat down on the broad sill, with the tulip snout for company, and curled her legs up under her, and began to watch the street. People came and went past the Dolphin House: sailors and craftsmen and merchants, a lady on a white mule, with a footboard for her feet and servants running ahead to clear the way, a red-faced man with a couple of hounds in leash, a black-robed friar from the nearby monastery, shuffling along in his flapping sandals, a strolling ballad-monger with a rose in his cap.

From the workshop below came the clash of the great sledge and the ring of the light hand-hammer, where Uncle Gideon and his men were at work on a suit of tilting armour. Tamsyn would like to have gone down to watch them, but one of the very strictest rules of the Dolphin House was that none of the children was allowed into the workshop but by special invitation—except, of course, to pass through it to the front door or the kitchen. Just once or twice she *had* been allowed into the workshop, and once Uncle Gideon had opened the great chest carved with coats of arms and Tudor roses where he kept the finest of his swords, and shown her a sword which he had not made himself at all, but which was his greatest treasure. It had a hilt of gold and age-darkened ivory, and a slender curved blade of blue steel on which the light played in a queer, steaky way, as it does on watered silk, and the grip was so small that it almost fitted Tamsyn's hand, and no grown man could have used it comfortably. Uncle Gideon had told her that it had been forged in Damascus two hundred years ago, for an Arab master, and that the grip was so small because Arabs had narrower hands than Englishmen. He had told her, too, that only the swordsmiths of Damascus forged blades of that strangely watered steel, which was why they were called damask blades. 'Damask blades, and the damask roses in the King's garden, and the damask silk of your Aunt's best gown, they all come from Damascus in the first place,' he said, wrapping his treasure in its silken case and putting it away again in the carved chest.

Tamsyn had loved that sword, and she would like to have gone downstairs to ask if she could see it again. But she had not been invited. Aunt Deborah had most particularly said to Uncle Gideon just before she went out, 'Now don't have that child down in the workshop; it's very hot and draughty down there, and she *has* got such a cold.'

So there was nothing for poor Tamsyn to do but sit on the parlour window-sill and poke dismally at her loose tooth, while her cold got worse every moment, as a cold always does when you are bored and miserable; for the cheering-up effect of the tulip snout had worn off after a little while.

But quite soon Meg the Kitchen came thumping upstairs with Bunch at her heels, and carrying a platter which she put down on the table beside the bowl of walnuts that always stood there in the walnut season. 'Here's your afternoons,' said Meg, 'and I've let you have it on the Bow Plate, so don't you break it!'

The Bow Plate was a great treasure, and only used for special treats. It had many-coloured flowers painted on it, and a lovely blue and rose and emerald bird in the middle which you only saw after you had eaten what was on the plate. This time the Bow Plate had two green figs on it, and instead of the usual brown bread, a little pastry man. A very smart little pastry man, with currant eyes and currant buttons on his doublet, who was still warm from the bake-oven.

'There!' said Meg the Kitchen. 'Now say I never give you nothing!'

'But I don't,' said Tamsyn. 'Truly I don't! And thank you *very* much, Meg.'

So Meg stumped down to her kitchen again, but Bunch stayed with Tamsyn, and she gave him the legs of the pastry man because she was so glad to see him. Then she ate the rest of the pastry man, biting on the loose tooth all the time, although it hurt, because the more you eat on a loose tooth the sooner it comes out. She did try cracking one of the walnuts on it, but that was really too painful, and after a moment or two she gave up the attempt, and put the walnut back in the bowl. The bite-marks did not really show. Then she ate the figs; they were showing bursty-pink through their green skins and beautifully sweet and slishy, only she couldn't taste them very well because of her cold. And after she had gathered up all the crumbs and eaten them, too, and blown her nose again, she decided to go up to Kit's Castle for a change.

So she kilted up her skirts, and went upstairs, with Bunch scampering ahead of her, round and round and up and up. At the top Bunch turned, wagging his tail so hard that his head wagged too, and kissed her very kindly with his warm, wet tongue, because he had a soft heart and knew that she had a cold and a loose tooth and was miserable.

'Oh, Bunch, darlin'!' said Tamsyn; and she sat down on the top step and cuddled him.

He was warm and wriggly and affectionate, and he seemed to like being cuddled, so she went on cuddling him, and they went on sitting on the top step and loving each other, until after a time they heard Piers calling up the stairs, 'Tamsy, where are you?'

Bunch and Tamsyn both pricked up their ears, and Bunch made a little pleased whining in his throat, as well as he could with being so tightly cuddled, and Tamsyn called back, 'I'm up here, in Kit's Castle.'

Then they heard footsteps running upstairs, and Piers' head came into view round the curve of the staircase. 'Hallo,' said Piers, coming to a halt and looking up at the forlorn-looking couple on the top step.

'Hullo,' said Tamsyn rather dolefully, peering down at him and still cuddling Bunch.

'How's your cold, Tamsy?'

'Beasterly!' said Tamsyn.

'Poor old lady!' said Piers, and he came on up the stairs.

Tamsyn sat quite firmly on the top step, cuddling Bunch round his soft neck. ''Tisn't time for you to stop work yet,' she told him dismally.

'Father's let me off work early, so I've come to keep you company,' said Piers. 'And if you would just stop roosting on the top step for a moment, I could come up.'

Tamsyn scrambled to her feet in a hurry, pulling Bunch after her. She had thought that Piers had only come to inquire for her cold, and that when he had inquired he would go away again; but if he had come to keep her company, that was quite different. So Piers came up the last three stairs, and Tamsyn stood and watched him, forlorn, but not quite so forlorn as she had been before he came.

'I have a loose tooth, too,' she said. 'It hurts.'

Piers said, 'Well, I'm afraid I can't do much about the cold, but I think I might be able to do something about the tooth. Come over to the window and show me.'

Tamsyn had a sudden sinking feeling in her inside. She did not want anyone to do anything about her tooth, she wanted it just to come out of its own accord as quickly as possible. But she never thought for an instant of disobeying Piers, so she took a deep breath and squared her shoulders, and followed him over to the window.

Piers turned her round to face the grey, drizzly light, and said, 'Open your mouth, Tamsy.'

Tamsyn opened it.

'Which tooth is it?'

Tamsyn pointed out the tooth. 'This one,' she said—at least she tried to say 'this one', but it is not easy to speak clearly with your mouth wide open, and so it sounded more like 'ich ung'.

'I see,' said Piers. He made no dreadful arrangements of thread or anything of that sort; he simply put his finger and thumb very gently into Tamsyn's mouth, and gave a little quick jerk. Tamsyn let out a surprised squawk—and he held up the tooth for her to see. 'Out!' said Piers, looking at her with his slow, grave smile. 'Good girl!'

Tamsyn gazed at the tooth, and heaved a sigh of relief. '*Thank* you, Piers,' she said.

He gave it into her hand, and warned her, 'Don't lose it, or you'll not get your penny from the Good People.'

So Tamsyn put it very carefully into her hanging pocket. You see, when any of the Dolphin House children shed a tooth they always put it in a little dish full of water beside the bowl of cream which Meg the Kitchen set outside the back door every night for the Good People, and in the morning the tooth would be gone, and there would be a bright new silver penny in its place. It was a great relief to Tamsyn to have got rid of the tooth (and really it hadn't hurt at all in coming out), and it was very nice to think that tomorrow she would have a silver penny for it.

When she had stowed the tooth away safely, Piers said, 'Now what shall we do?'

Tamsyn didn't answer; she just stood gazing up at him, hopefully, with her head a little on one side, like a puppy that thinks you may be going to throw a ball for it, because she saw that he knew exactly what they were going to do, and that whatever it was, it would be lovely.

For a long breathless moment Piers didn't say any more; only he had quite stopped being the quiet, everyday Piers who was learning to be a swordsmith, and become the exciting Piers who told wonderful stories and could make you see everything he told about. His eyes were dancing bright, and his hair looked more like the ruffled feathers of a bird every instant, and he stood with arms akimbo, rocking gently on his heels and looking down at Tamsyn. And Tamsyn stood on tiptoe with excitement, and gazed up at Piers—waiting.

And suddenly Kit's Castle put aside its everyday self, too, and became an enchanted place where simply anything could happen.

Then Piers spoke in a thrilling voice. 'Mistress Tamsyn,' he said, 'the whole evening is before us; therefore we are about to launch the *Dolphin and Joyous Venture* and sail her into the Golden West.'

'Oh!' said Tamsyn, 'could we?'

'There is nothing that we cannot do,' said Piers. 'We will see the marvels of the New World and sail the golden Spanish Seas! We will trade for cedarwood and cinnamon and milky pearls, and fight Spaniards.' (England and Spain were not very friendly just then, though not so unfriendly as later on, so of course Spanish ships were the best sort to fight.)

'Oh!' said Tamsyn again. 'Let's start now, this moment.'

Piers said, 'First we must build our ship.' And before the words were out of his mouth he had sprung into action, flinging back the lid of the play-chest and scattering everything that was in it far and wide, in search of the things he needed.

Tamsyn flew to help him, and between them they built their ship in a wonderfully short time; at least, Piers did most of the actual building, while Tamsyn helped and held things and fetched and carried. First he chalked the outline of the decks on the floor, and made a mast out of the longest quarter-staff, by stepping it in a bran-filled barrel that had been made ready for apples. Bunch was in the way rather at first, because of wanting to help; but when Piers moved the apple-barrel he found a mouse-hole behind it, and decided to have a nice mouse-hunt instead. Bunch liked mouse-hunting because he didn't have to work hard, as he did if he was taken into the fields and hunted rabbits. All you have to do, to mouse-hunt, is to lie down comfortably with your nose against a mouse-hole, and bark. That is what Bunch did. He always seemed to expect the mice to come out, if he only went on barking long enough. Of course they never did, and so he never caught any; but he didn't seem to mind, so everybody was satisfied.

Piers contrived a sail from one of the old pieces of cloth in the play-chest, and stood back an instant to admire it, before diving into the play-chest again. 'Guns!' he cried, with his head inside the chest. 'Guns, for the love of Heaven! How can we sail seas swarming with Spanish Corsairs, without guns for our defence? Culverin and falcons—we must have proper armament!' He came out triumphantly with the battered pewter pot, which he set on its side on a box in the waist of the ship. Then he dived into the play-chest again, and brought out the dried sea-horse. 'Behold the figure-head of the *Dolphin and Joyous Venture*!' he announced, and propped it up in the bows of the ship. Lastly he fetched the lovely chart from his garret and put it in the stern, where the Master's cabin would be in a real ship. Then he took Tamsyn's hand and they stepped carefully over the chalk outline on to the deck of the *Dolphin and Joyous Venture*.

'Now,' said Piers, 'we must make a tremendously strong Believing-magic. Shut your eyes while I speak the Words of Power, and hold tight, and believe as hard as ever you know how, that the *Dolphin and Joyous Venture* is a real ship!'

So Tamsyn shut her eyes, screwing them up so tight that she could see globes of coloured light against the darkness, and believed —and believed—and believed, as hard as ever she knew how, so that it was like winding something up very tight inside her, while Piers recited in a slow and thrilling whisper:

> 'Earth, Water, Wind and Fire,
> Merlin, Huon of Bordoux,
> Betelgeuse and Belatrix
> Make—our—ship—REAL.'

Then she opened her eyes very wide indeed.

Now, if anybody else had been in Kit's Castle, looking on, the chalk outline and the apple-barrel and all the other things would have seemed to them to be just as they were before Piers spoke the Words of Power. But to Piers and Tamsyn everything was quite different, and to them the *Dolphin and Joyous Venture* was as real as any ship in the Port of London, because they had made a Believing-magic about her. It is wonderful what you can do with a Believing-magic, if only you believe hard enough.

Kit's Castle was gone, and the fine grey rain across the windows turned to morning sunshine and the slap and sparkle of water along the sides of the tall ship, and her masts towered up and up, with all their delicate cobweb rigging strung between, and their loosened sails gleaming against the sky. The dinted pewter pot became the culverin and falcons and murdering-pieces that all merchant ships carried in those days, to defend themselves against pirates and the ships of Spain; and the dried sea-horse was the lovely carved and painted figure-head beneath the bowsprit; and Piers was the Master and Tamsyn was the Master's Mate.

The anchor was weighed and the sails sheeted home, and the ship began to move, slipping through the water. Tamsyn felt her lift as the seas took her, and she heeled over gently to the wind and bore away for the open sea.

The Great Adventure had begun!

'Westward Ho!' cried the Master. 'A course set for the Golden Indies; and who knows what adventure we shall meet with before we drop anchor in London River again, Mister Mate!'

England faded into the summer mists astern, and they ran on under full sail, south and west through the blue emptiness of the Atlantic, until the great spouting whales that they had seen at first gave place to rainbow-winged flying-fish, and dolphins leapt and tumbled in the wake of the ship; and on until they came at last to the Golden Indies. Here the water was as deeply blue as larkspur flowers, and between Cuba and Jamaica and Hispaniola the countless little islands with their white coral beaches and palm-feathered crests and brilliant flowers were as bright as the jewelled feathers of a humming-bird's breast, just as they were in the wonderful chart in the Master's cabin. And the *Dolphin and Joyous Venture* sailed on among these dream islands, trading as she went for cinnamon and cedar-wood and milk-white pearls (for in those days all explorers and adventurers were merchants, and all merchants were explorers and adventurers).

The Master pointed out all the wonders of the Golden Indies to the spellbound Mate, so that she could see them as plain as plain; fishes of gold and vermilion, azure and flaming emerald that darted and hovered among waving forests of fronded seaweed, through water so clear that you could look down and watch the shadows of the ripples on the white coral sand five fathoms below; giant crabs that climbed trees to eat the sweet nuts that grew at the top; strange and lovely birds, pink as the sunset, who flew with their long legs trailing out behind them as the herons flew at home; brown people with strange patterns pricked on their skins, and collars of shark's teeth and brilliant feathers round their necks, who came down boldly to trade with the English ship. All these the Master showed to the Mate, as well as mermaids and sea-serpents; and he showed her, too, the stately Spanish galleons that came and went among the islands and through the Gulf of Darien, with towering sides and spread of snowy canvas that seemed to touch the sky.

Then they sailed south again, through golden seas along the golden shores of the New World, until they came to the mouth of a river so broad that it was like a sea; and the Master said that it was the Orenoque, so they ran the Dolphin far up it, to explore.

The Mate knew all that country of old, for it was the country of the lovely chart. There were the wide plains and snow-capped mountain ranges, there were the forests of flowering trees with birds of pink and white and crimson, purple and azure and golden-green like living gems among their branches; there were the black bears and firebreathing dragons and milk-white deer, and the natives with strange bird head-dresses who were all quite friendly in a stately sort of way, if you spoke to them nicely. And when night came down, the forests were all a-sparkle with fire-flies, as though the stars had fallen out of heaven to dance among the trees.

'And over there,' said the Master— 'somewhere over there beyond those purple mountains and the blue ones beyond again—is Manoa, the Golden City that the Spaniards call El Dorado. They do say it is more glorious even than the ancient city of the Incas used to be, in the days before Pizarro and his cut-throats conquered Peru and killed the Inca Atahualpa.'

He told her how a younger brother of Atahualpa had fled from Peru, followed by all that was left of his army, and carrying with him the ancient treasure of the Incas, the golden treasure of the Sun God, that was great enough to ransom every King and Emperor of this world ten times over; and how he had vanquished all the country between the head-waters of the Amazon and Orenoque, and built his great city in the midst of a sacred lake, a city all of gold, glorious as the sun; and how he sat there to this day, a Golden King among his Golden Court, waiting for the fulfilment of an ancient prophecy: that one day heroes would come out of the east and head him back through the jungle to Peru and help him to win back his ancient kingdom.

'And nobody knows where it is?' asked the Mate, when the Master had finished.

'Nobody,' said the Master, 'only that it is somewhere beyond those mountains; and we haven't time to look for it, just now.'

'Let's come back and look, one day,' said the Mate.

'Surely,' said the Master.

So they returned to the *Dolphin and Joyous Venture,* and set her on a course for home.

But the greatest adventure of all was still to come; for hardly had the coast of the New World dropped over the skyline, than they sighted a great ship.

They had sighted many ships before, and none of them had offered to interfere with the *Dolphin,* but almost at once they saw that this one had altered course, and was heading towards them.

'Oh! Could it be pirates?' cried the Mate. 'Do you think it could be pirates?'

The Master shaded his eyes with his hand and gazed into the distance. 'I don't know,' he said. 'I don't like it. These are Spanish waters, and every Spaniard turns pirate when it suits him.'

'Shall we fight?' asked the Mate, breathlessly.

'If she tries to interfere with us, we shall most assuredly fight,' said the Master. 'Look! She's coming straight down-wind on us; a Spanish galleon, by the looks of her!' Then he let out the most tremendous yell. 'By Cock and Pie! It's the *Santa Marguerita* herself! *And* she's trying to head us off! Oh no, you don't, Don Spaniard! The seas are free to all! Hold her to her course, helmsman. Trumpeter, sound to Quarters. Clear the decks for action! Run out the guns!' And he came leaping down from the poop, to be half a gun's crew, with the Mate for the other half.

The Mate's heart was almost bursting with excitement as she and the Master laboured to run out and load their culverin. Nets were rigged out to protect the gun's crews from falling spars, and the two ships bore down upon each other, until she could see the golden banner of Castile fluttering from the galleon's poop, and her gilded sides towering up with all her guns grinning in the sunlight. Then came a puff of smoke and the roar of a cannon, and a round shot plunged into the water just beyond the bows of the *Dolphin and Joyous Venture*.

'Thinks we shall surrender, does he?' said the Master between his teeth; and a moment later, 'Fire!'

There was a roar and a flash, and the little *Dolphin* leapt and quivered from stem to stern as she fired into the towering sides of the galleon and bore away to avoid punishment, before the *Santa Marguerita's* guns roared in reply.

It was a most tremendous fight! The great *Santa Marguerita* towered over the little *Dolphin*—like Goliath over David, as the Master said— but the English ship was quicker than the Spaniard, as English ships generally were. She fired, and swung away to reload, and came round again to pour in another broadside, and another, and another, in answer to the crashing broadside of the enemy, until the air was full of the thunder of the guns and the acid smoke of them and the yelling of the English and Spaniards, and the tall hull of the *Santa Marguerita* was battered and holed. But still her guns roared and she did not surrender; and the main topmast of the *Dolphin* was almost shot in two at the heel, so that she had to draw off to make it secure.

Then the Master decided on a very bold stroke, and as soon as the mast was secured he sent his ship straight down once more upon the enemy.

'St. George for Merry England!' roared the English seaman, as the little *Dolphin*, with drums beating and the red cross of St. George fluttering from her poop, ran straight in under the enemy's guns. 'Hold her to her course, helmsman,' shouted the Master. 'Now —ready about!' and the *Dolphin* came about like a live thing on the opposite tack, passing right under the towering stern of the *Santa Marguerita*.

'Fire!' yelled the Master; and once again the *Dolphin's* culverin flamed and crashed, and a hail of clothyard arrows and smaller shot swept the galleon's poop clear. Her stern-walk crumpled in, the mizzen mast went down with a crash, and the golden banner of Castile hung in shreds. The great ship shivered and began to swing helplessly round. 'Look!' cried the Master of the *Dolphin*. 'We must have damaged her tiller: she's falling up into the wind!'

'What do we do now?' demanded the Mate.

'Wait. She's getting under control again,' said the Master. 'Oh, but she's had enough. See, she's drawing off. Let her go. She'll be lucky if she ever makes port in *that* mess.'

'Hurrah!' yelled the English, thronging the reeking decks of the *Dolphin and Joyous Venture*.

The Mate straightened up from her almost red-hot gun. 'That'll learn the King of Spain!' she said blithely, as she watched the *Santa Marguerita,* the pride of the Spanish fleet, staggering out of the fight.

There was a great deal to be done aboard the *Dolphin* and *Joyous Venture;* the littered decks to be cleared, wounded to be tended and the shot-holes stopped up, and the damaged topmast to be properly set to rights; but it was all done at last, and then they put her triumphantly back on her course for England.

And almost at once they heard the front door slam, and Aunt Deborah's voice somewhere in the house.

The Master, with great presence of mind, cried, 'Home at last, and a fair wind all the way!' and sprang ashore with the Mate following him. Instantly the Believing-magic came undone, the tall masts of the *Dolphin and Joyous Venture* dwindled into a quarter staff in an apple barrel, and they were back in Kit's Castle in the twilight, with the chilly rain drizzling in through the windows and Bunch still lying hopefully in front of his mouse-hole; and the Master was Piers, and Mate was Tamsyn. And the shadows that had begun to crowd out from the corners and behind barrels and boxes to watch and listen, crept back again to their places before anyone noticed that they had been out of them.

'Adventure all over, Tamsy,' said Piers. 'Let's get all this cleared away before anyone comes up.'

Tamsyn knew exactly what he meant. Neither of them could bear to think of the Almost-Twins seeing the ship that they had built, because to them she was lovely, but to the Almost-Twins she would be just a collection of boxes and pewter pots, and they would think her funny. So they set to work in a great hurry, taking the gallant little Dolphin to pieces, and tumbling everything back into the play-chest. Then Piers put away his lovely chart, and there was nothing to show what they had been doing—nothing at all but the outline of a ship drawn in chalk on the floor, which would not rub out very well; but it didn't much matter.

Then Piers and Tamsyn stood and looked at each other, both a little breathless.

'Well, it was a good adventure, wasn't it, Tamsy?' said Piers.

'Oh, it was lovcrly!' whispered Tamsyn. 'It was the most *enormously* exciting adventure. And I do like adventures.'

Piers smiled his slow, grave smile, and said, 'If—if I was going to sea, I'd come back when I got to be a Master, and then you could marry me and come with me on my voyages. Ships' Masters often take their wives with them—and we'd have lots of adventures together.'

'Oh!' breathed Tamsyn, gripping her hands together. 'Would you? Would we? Really and truly?' And she was quite as pleased as though Piers really *was* going to sea.

'Really and truly,' said Piers, 'if I was going to sea. But we'd better be going downstairs now, before somebody comes to look for us. Come along, old lady.'

So they went down and down and round and round into the parlour, where the candles had been lit and Meg was setting the table for supper, and all the family were gathered together.

'Well, poppet, you don't look nearly so coldy,' said Aunt Deborah the moment she saw Tamsyn. 'And what have you and Piers been doing with yourselves?'

'I had a loose tooth, and Piers pulled it out, Aunt Deborah,' said Tamsyn, taking the tooth out of her hanging pocket and holding it up triumphantly for everyone to see.

'Oh, my poor poppet!' said Aunt Deborah. 'Don't forget to put it out for the Good People tonight.'

And presently she went upstairs to put Littlest to bed, and Beatrix went upstairs to take off her cloak. And when Beatrix came back, she told the whole family scornfully, 'I know what they've been doing. They've been playing ships! There's an outline of one chalked on Kit's Castle floor.'

'Oh, don't be a zany!' Giles said, helping himself to walnuts. 'Piers isn't any good at that sort of thing.'

Tamsyn looked across the parlour at Piers in a surprised sort of way; because it seemed so very queer that that was what people should think they had been doing—just playing ships. It had all been so much more real than that; she could remember so well the lovely lift of the *Dolphin's* deck as the seas took her, and the birds of white and pink and crimson among the forests of the New World, and the roar of the *Santa Marguerita's* guns.

And Piers looked across the parlour at Tamsyn; and they smiled at each other in a shared-secret sort of way, because nobody knew what they had been doing that evening, whatever anybody might think—nobody in all the world.

Before she went to bed that night Tamsyn put her tooth in the little dish of water outside the back door for the Good People; and when she went out first thing in the morning, to collect her penny, there it was, bright and new in the bottom of the dish. And there, floating above it, was a little ship! A ship made of a walnut shell, with a splinter of wood for a mast and a scrap of parchment for a sail, and a tiny squiggle of silver wire at her stem that Tamsyn knew at once for a dolphin! She never showed that little ship to anybody, except Piers. You have to be very careful who you show a gift from the fairies to, and Tamsyn knew that quite well.

7 *A Tale for Hallowe'en*

The weeks went by, and Tamsyn's tulip had three milky-green leaves and something that looked as though it might be a flower-bud, deep down among them, so that Aunt Deborah said, 'Deary me, I do believe it's going to flower by Christmas after all.' But of course Tamsyn had known all along that it *would* flower at Christmas, because the Wise Woman had said so.

It was autumn now, and on fine mornings every leaf and grass-blade in the little garden behind the Dolphin House was furred with hoar-frost round the edge, and there were swirly feathery frost-flowers on the parlour window-panes, the Surrey Hills were blue as the flowers of the bitter-sweet; and on fine evenings all the world was full of the smell of wood-smoke, and the sun went down in a pink-flushed sky behind Westminster. On other days the thick, dun-coloured fog rolled up the river, and even found its way indoors, so that when the candles were lighted in the evenings, they burned with golden haloes round them like the ones worn by saints in old pictures. There began to be sellers of russet apples and hot chestnuts in the streets, and the blue, frosty dusk came earlier every evening, so that the Dolphin House children no longer played in the garden or even in Kit's Castle after supper, but drew their stools close round the fire in the parlour, and plagued their mother for stories.

For long, dark evenings in the fire-glow are the times for telling old stories; and of all the evenings in the year, Hallowe'en is the very best—except perhaps Christmas Eve.

This particular Hallowe'en was cold and frosty, and the fire of beech logs burned clear red all through, just right for baking apples and roasting chestnuts. Supper was over, and the children were tired of playing Hot-cockles and 'Cheeses' and everybody had gathered close around the fire; Aunt Deborah and Uncle Gideon in their own tall-backed chairs at either side, and Piers and Tamsyn and Bunch and the Almost-Twins perched on stools or squatting on the warm, rush-deep floor between them. There was a delicious smell and a delicious sizzling of the little red apples roasting among the hot ash, and Giles had just put a handful of chestnuts to roast among them. The candles had all been snuffed out—firelight is quite enough on Hallowe'en as everyone knows—and the warm leaping light of the burning logs sent queer, fantastic shadows licking up the walls almost as far as the ceiling: Uncle Gideon's and Aunt Deborah's, and between them the children's shadows, and a little upright shadow with pricked ears that was Bunch's. Uncle Gideon had been reading his best-beloved book out of the oak chest, the one which was called the Iliad; but he had stopped reading now, and closed the book, and sat with one finger between the pages to keep his place, gazing into the red heart of the fire. Aunt Deborah was mending a pile of hose—Uncle Gideon's black ones and Piers' brown ones, Giles' green ones, and a wee scarlet pair that belonged to Littlest. Tamsyn was making a partlet strip to be a Christmas present for Uncle Gideon. You see, none of the Dolphin House children had very much pocket-money, and so they made most of their Christmas presents themselves, quite often in full view of the person it was going to be given to, who was, of course, in honour bound not to look. Partlet strips were things men and boys used to wear round their necks before ruffs came into fashion. This was one of fine holland embroidered all over in black silk with a vine-leaf design in all the different stitches Tamsyn knew how to do. Neither she nor Aunt Deborah could see to sew very much, but every time the fire leapt up they put in two or three more stitches, and when it sank again, they just sat.

Nobody else was doing anything at all.

'Mother,' said Giles suddenly, 'tell us a story.'

Everybody looked up hopefully at Aunt Deborah, and Aunt Deborah laid down the little red stocking she was darning, and said, 'Very well, my poppets. What story shall I tell you?'

'You *always* tell us about Young Tam Lin on Hallowe'en, Mother,' said Giles reproachfully. 'You know you do.'

'Yes, I do, don't I?' said Aunt Deborah. She looked down at the red stocking in her lap with a queer little smile that was half glad and half sorry. Then she looked up again, and said, 'I've told that story every Hallowe'en since—since Kit was a little tiny boy, he always loved it so much—and surely you must all know it off by heart by this time. Wouldn't you like another story for a change?'

Piers shook his head. 'Hallowe'en wouldn't be Hallowe'en without Young Tam Lin, Mother,' he said, 'really it wouldn't. Besides, Tamsy hasn't heard it at all.'

'Very well,' said Aunt Deborah again, and she rolled the little red stocking into a ball and put it with the others, while everybody drew closer to the fire in an expectant way. 'Come closer still,' said Aunt Deborah, leaning down towards them. 'Come very close, my dears, for it is not wise to speak loud of the Good People, on this night of all the year.'

Everyone cast quick glances behind them, at the queer, crowding shadows (shadows are not quite the same at Hallow-tide, as they are on other nights of the year), and shivered with a delicious sort of creepiness and crowded closer still into the fire-glow that was painting golden roses on the soft grey stuff of Aunt Deborah's skirt.

'When I was a little girl,' began Aunt Deborah, 'there was an old friend of my father's, one of those who went north with the Princess Margaret when she was sent as a bride to the Scottish King. There were gay doings at Holyrood for the Royal Wedding, and at the dancing in the great hall he met a Highland gentlewoman, and they were wed, and he brought her south with him. And oh! but she was lovely! Tall and dark, with the great eyes of her set slantwise in her face as though she were a faun. I have often wondered whether all the Highland women are as beautiful as she was. Well, so she used to come often to visit my mother—I think she was lonely in the south—and sometimes she would tell me stories in her soft voice that had an odd lilt to it, always stories of her own country. One of her stories was about Young Tam Lin, and this is how she used to tell it, as nearly as I can remember.'

'High among the hills of Carterhaugh there was once a little lonely well. Soft green turf rimmed it round, and the long sprays of the wild rose arched over it; and in the hottest summer the water never sank but a little way below the broken grey stones of the well-curb. Yet no one ever drew water there, and no one ever passed that way after dusk, and if ever a maiden found herself near the spot while herding sheep in the hills, she would leave a gift beside the broken well-curb and hurry away as fast as her feet would carry her; for it was fairy ground.

'But once, long, long ago, before even our grandmothers were born, a maiden did come to the Fairy Well of Carterhaugh. The Chieftain's daughter, she was, and her name was Janot, and ever since she was a baby the old nurse who brought her up had warned her against the Fairy Well, as every nurse and every mother in Selkirkshire warned her bairns. But she was a wild lass, like a hawk of the sea-cliffs, and her eyes as blue as the harebells and her long, straight hair as yellow as the broom; and there came a day when she grew tired of warnings and hungry for adventure, so she kicked off her shoes and braided her yellow hair and kilted her green kirtle to her knee, and slipped away from her companions in the castle garden. Before they knew that she was gone she was off and away to Carterhaugh as fast as her bare feet would carry her. On she went, by sheep-tracks of smooth turf, through seas of uncurling bracken and young bilberries, following ever the river Ettrick until she came to Carterhaugh and up over the moors to the Fairy Well.

'Oh, but it was wild and lonely up there, with the larks singing in the wide skies, and the whaups crying, and the land dropping away from her feet to the blue hills of the Border Country. And all at once Janot was afraid, and just for a moment she thought that she would take the gold pin from her gown and leave it for a gift to the Fairy Kind, and go home quickly, as she had come. But she was not one to turn away from a thing because she was afraid; so she bent forward across the well-curb, and broke off a long wild-rose spray that arched above it. There were two pink blossoms upon the spray, and as she broke it off, the petals fell from one of them, as is the way of wild roses when their branch is shaken. She leaned forward to watch the five petals floating in the dark water, and there was her own face looking up at her from the depths—aye, and another face looking over her shoulder! A thin face it was, and dark enough to startle any maid.

'For the time that it might take your heart to beat twice, Janot never moved. Then she turned slowly from the well-curb, still holding the rose-switch in her hand. Close beside her on the green-sward stood a brave young gallant, clad all in green, from his close-fitting hose to his feathered bonnet. And oh, but he was bonny, despite his black hair and his wan, dark face; there was a cleft to his chin and a quirk to his eyebrow, and the eyes of him were bright and grey.

' "And why do you pick my roses, Janot?" asked the young man.

'And Janot lifted her chin disdainfully, and, "The roses are free to all," she said.

' "Ah, but they are not. The roses belong to Themselves who own the well," said the young man. "The roses are mine."

' "Then you will be one of Themselves—one of the Lordly People?" says she, breathing fast, for she was afraid. For answer he bowed his head on his breast; and seeing him standing there with bowed head and no word to say, her fear left her, and she said, "You have called me by my name; will you not tell me yours, fairy though you be?"

' "I am called Tam Lin," said the young man, and, as he spoke, he doffed his bonnet to her so low that it swept the fern.

'Ach well, for a while and a little while they talked together, there by the well, until the shadows began to lengthen, and the larks dropped out of the heavens. Then Tam Lin said, "Now you must go home, Janot, or your father will be seeking you and fearing you lost. My heart is sore to let you go, but there is no help for it, no help at all." And he took her hand and turned her towards her home; and suddenly her hand was gone from hers, and when she turned, there was no one beside her—only five rose-petals floated on the dark well-water and a whaup rose crying into the evening sky.

'So Janot went home, barefoot through the young bracken as she had come. She carried the wild-rose spray with its one pink blossom with her, but she left her heart behind her on Carterhaugh with young Tam Lin. And ever as she went, there was a wild weeping within her, for it is an ill thing to give your heart to the Fairy Kind, who have none to give in return.

'The summer ripened and wore away, and Janot worked at her tapestry frame as skilfully as ever, and played ball as merrily with her ladies among the rose trees in the castle garden, and danced as lightly in the great hall when the candles were lighted. But those who knew her best saw that she was not happy. They saw that her laughter never touched her eyes, and they saw her turn ever towards Carterhaugh when she thought that none was by; and her father, the Chieftain, thought, "Maybe she would be happier wed."

'So one day he said to her, "Janot, you are grown up now, and it is time that you were wed. Is there any man near to your heart, my daughter? For if there is, and he is worthy, you shall surely have him."

' "No," she said, and laughed, for how should she tell her father, "it is no man that is near to my heart, but one of the Lordly People"?

'The summer grew to autumn, and still Janot turned to Carterhaugh when she thought that none was by, and still her laughter never touched her eyes. Then one day her father went to her, where she sat alone in her bower. "Janet," said he, "is there still no man near your heart?"

' "None," says she.

' "Then I shall choose a husband for you, for it is time that you were wed."

'Up sprang his daughter to her feet. "You may choose to your heart's content," says she, "but I will have none of your choice. There's not a man among the lordlings in your hall that I would wed if he were the last man in Scotland."

'Then the old Chief was angry, though he was a kindly man. "You shall wed whom I choose, and *when* I choose, Janot," said he. "I have been patient with you all the summer, and I'll be patient but a short time longer." And out he went, and slammed the bower door behind him.

'For a while after he was gone, Janot stood where he had left her, as still as the grey standing-stones on the moor above, and then she cast herself face down upon her bed and wept most bitterly; for it is an ill thing to give your heart to the Fairy Kind, who have neither heart to give in return nor soul to walk in God's good heaven. Yet she could not quite believe that it was so with Tam Lin. Surely none of the Fairy Folk had eyes as true as he, surely, surely . . .

'Up she sprang and went to her mirror. She dressed her yellow hair and braided it with gold-work as though she were going to her wedding; but she kicked off her shoes of fine Cordovan leather and kilted her green kirtle to her knee, and she went down the winding stair and out by a postern gate, and set off and away like a winged thing towards Carterhaugh.

'The bracken that had been freshly green when last she came that way was golden-tawny now, and swayed to her waist as she passed through. Past sky-reflecting moorland pools she sped, down beside the Ettrick, and up and over the dun moors of Carterhaugh like a deer with the hounds behind her, until at last she came to the Fairy Well.

'There were no blossoms on the brier that arched above the water now, but the rose-hips shone scarlet in the autumn sunshine, and hastily Janot broke off a spray, just as she had done before. Five shrivelled yellow leaves fell from it, and she leaned forward eagerly to watch them floating on the still water. Her own face looked back at her from below the floating leaves; and just as before, the dark face of Tam Lin looked over her shoulder.

'Round she turned from the well-curb, and there stood Tam Lin beside her, just as she had remembered him, from green-shod foot to bonnet feather.

' "Why do you pull the wild-rose spray, Janot?" asked he. "And why have you come back to Carterhaugh?"

' "My father is for choosing me a husband," said Janot.

' "And is there no man that is near to your heart?"

' "None save you yourself, Tam Lin," said Janot proudly. "That is why I come to Carterhaugh. That is why I pull the wild-rose spray."

' "It is an ill thing for any maid to give her heart to the Fairy Kind, who have none to give in fair exchange," said Tam Lin, with his eyes upon her face.

'Then Janot gave him back look for look, and "Tam Lin," she cried, "if ever you were mortal child, I pray you tell me now! I have heard of children taken by Themselves—was it so with you? If ever you heard church-bells ringing, if ever you knew a prayer, tell me; for it is an ill thing indeed, if I have given my heart to the Fairy Kind."

' "I will tell you," said Tam Lin, and he took her hands and held them close. "And I will tell you the truth, Janot. My father was a knight and my mother was a lady. I was born and christened and reared and trained as any other good knight's son. But one cold, dark day as I rode home from the hunting, my horse stumbled, and I was thrown. I was thrown on Fairy Ground, Janot, and Themselves took me to be a knight of theirs, under the hollow hills."

'Then Janot's heart was glad, yet troubled too, and she asked, "What need had the Proud Folk to take you from the world of the Sun? Have they not knights enough of their own, in Fairydom?"

' "Oh, they have knights enough of their own," said Tam Lin, and laughed; but his laugh had a dreary ring to it that set the whaups crying. "Do you not know that once in seven years the Fairy Kind must give one of their number to the power of Hell?"

'Then Janot cried out, and her face was white as the first snow of winter. "Will they give *you*?" she cried, and her voice wailed over the moors like a plover calling rain. "Is *that* why they took you to be their knight in the hollow hills?"

' "That is why they took me. That is always their reason for taking human children," said Tam Lin. "And the seven years are almost up, Janot; but you can save me if you will."

' "Tell me!" she demanded. "Tell me! There is nothing in all the world or beyond it that I will not do."

' "It is a terrible thing that you must face, and a hard thing that you must do; and if you fail we shall both be lost to all eternity."

'But she said, "I am not afraid." And she waited for him to tell her the thing that she must do.

' "Tonight is Hallowe'en," said Tam Lin, "and tonight at midnight the Fairy Folk will ride. And if you would win me away from them, you must be waiting here to take me as the cavalcade goes by."

' "But oh, Tam Lin, how shall I know you in the dark, and among all the knights of Fairydom?"

' "Here is how you shall know me," said Tam Lin, 'and this is what you shall do. You shall hide here in the shadow of the well-curb to watch the Court of Elfland pass, and there will be light for you to see by, moonshine and elf-glow. First you shall see the Queen, riding by her lone, in a gown of green, with gold-work round her hair, and her hair as yellow as yours, Janot, and her eyes as blue as yours. Then will come the ladies of the Court, riding all together, and when the last lady has gone by, look for the knights who follow hard behind. The first knight will ride a horse as black as midnight, and the second, a horse as brown as a polished chestnut, and the third, a horse as white as milk. Let the black go by, Janot, and let the brown go by, but run to the milk-white steed and pull his rider down, for the rider of the milk-white steed will be no one but myself. Then hold me—hold me tightly, for the Fairy Folk will not easily let me go; they'll turn me in your arms into many strange and hideous things, but remember always that it is I, Tam Lin, and hold me close, and do not be afraid, and I'll do you no harm. At the very last they'll turn me to a burning coal between your hands. Then throw me quickly into the well-water, and I shall be in Tam Lin's shape again. Then cover me with your green cloak, and I shall be safe from the Fairy Kind. I shall be your own true love, Janot, for ever and for always; this I swear."

' "I will be here," said Janot. "I will not fail you."

'Then Tam Lin kissed her once upon the brow and once upon the lips, and turned her towards her home. And suddenly his hand was gone from hers, and when she looked round, there was no one beside her—only five yellow leaves afloat in the well-water and a whaup crying above the hills. So she went home barefoot through the fern, as she had done before, and she carried the brier spray with her, but she left her heart on Carterhaugh with young Tam Lin.

'That night she went early to her bed, saying that she was tired; but as soon as her maidens left her she rose again and dressed, flung her wide green cloak around her shoulders, and stole down the winding stair and out by the postern gate. It was cold, cold and dark, for the moon was not yet risen, and already the turf was crisped with frost, and the brambles and the bracken seemed to clutch at her with little icy fingers as she fled by. But she came up and over the moors to Carterhaugh at last, and crouched down beside the curb of the Fairy Well.

'The moon was near to rising, and in a little while it lifted over the dark rim of the hills; the great red moon of the Fairy Kind, scarlet as hot coals on the edge of the sky. Slowly it swam up and up, growing paler as it rose, until all the moors were changed from black to glimmering silver under a glimmering silver sky. And Janot loosed her green cloak on her shoulders, for she knew that it was near to midnight.

'She did not see the Elf-throng in the distance; she did not know when they were drawing near, but suddenly she heard a bridle ring, and they were close upon her as she crouched there in the shadows of the Fairy Well. The silver of the moon was all about them, and their lanterns glowed like emeralds, so that she saw them clear. The Queen rode by, with white moonshine and green elf-light mingled in her hair, and she with locks as yellow as the broom and eyes as blue as the harebells of the glens; and all behind her rode her ladies in high, fantastic head-dresses and shadowy robes of green. Here a jewel flashed and there a horse's up-reared crest caught the light like the curve of a breaking wave, and there a filmy sleeve floated across the moon, and dark eyes glimmered and a red mouth laughed and a white hand fluttered on a bridle-rein. But Janot scarcely glanced that way, for she was looking always beyond them, for the knights who followed after. Many and many were the ladies of the Elf Queen's Court; but at last they had all gone by, and the knights came on behind. First there rode a knight in yellow on a great black horse, and next there rode a knight in scarlet red, on a horse of glossy brown, and then there came a knight clad all in green and mounted on a horse whose flanks shone white as milk beneath the trappings.

'Then up sprang Janot, and ran to the milk-white steed. She heard the thunder of his great round hoofs, and his mane blinded her as it flowed across her face, but her arms were fast about the rider, and she pulled him down. Then there rose a frightful shriek from all the Fairy Host, and Queen and courtiers and fairy steeds were gone from mortal sight into a great wind which swept and swirled around Janot. Great wings beat about her head and screaming voices deafened her and strange lights danced before her eyes; and in place of Tam Lin she was holding close against her a writhing, whipping, fork-tongued adder. Yet she remembered what her love had told her, and held fast to the hideous little thing; and next instant 'twas no longer an adder that she held, but a great, black bear with rending claws, and she was dragged to her knees, still clinging to its thick fur with all her strength, while still the wild wings beat about her head and the wild voices shrieked in her ears. Then, with a roar, the bear was changed into a lion, milky-toothed and red of eye, with foaming jaws and flame about its head, but she twisted her hands in its mane and clung with all her might until the ravening lion was become a red-hot bar of iron. Oh! but the cruel agony scorched her through and through, so that all her body seemed made of pain. But she cradled the glowing bar against her as tenderly as a mother cradles her babe, shielding it from the screaming things that tried to tear it from her. And suddenly it was changed to a burning coal that she held in her cupped hands, with the bright flames licking through her fingers.

'Then she whirled about with a cry, and flung the hot coal from her into the well, just as Tam Lin had bade her do. The wild wings ceased to beat about her head, and the screaming voices were stilled, and the strange lights flickered out; only the Fairy Wind still swept and swirled around her, and Tam Lin's hand and arm came over the well-curb and his head rose from the dark water.

' "Now cover me with your cloak, Janot," he cried. "Cover me quickly from their sight."

'And Janot slipped the cloak from off her shoulders and muffled him from sight as he climbed over the well-curb.

'All that night she sat beside him as he lay under her wide green cloak, and the frost was bitter cold, and the moon shone down over Carterhaugh so that all the moors were webbed with glimmering silver, save where the woods stood dark along the valleys. And all the while the Fairy Wind swooped about them out of a quiet sky, and the woods slept in the windless night below. But at last the dawn flushed golden in the east, and the rim of the sun slid up over the hills, and the Fairy Wind died down. Then Janot lifted the wide green cloak from off Tam Lin, and "Dear Heart, it is day," she said.

'They looked each into the other's eyes as the first golden finger of the sunlight touched the moors, and the larks were singing above them in the morning sky; and they knew that they were safe.

'And "I will be true-love to you, Janot, for ever and for always," said Tam Lin.

'So in a little while they went down from Carterhaugh, hand in hand, and turned towards Janot's home, but this time Tam Lin's hand remained in the hand of Janot, for he was free of the Fairy Kind.

'And that, my dears, is the end of the story.'

Everybody sat quite still for a moment after the story was over, and then Beatrix heaved a little, contented sigh, and said, 'I *do* like that story!'

'I wonder what Janot's father said when she brought Tam Lin home,' said Giles, fishing hot chestnuts out of the fire. 'I'll wager he was surprised—so surprised he nearly fell over backwards! I say, I wonder what he *did* say.'

Uncle Gideon smiled at the fire, and said in his quiet way, 'Do you know, I have always wondered the same thing. It must be a little surprising, even perhaps a little upsetting, to find that one's only child has brought home a perfectly strange bridegroom before breakfast.'

'I expect he was so pleased he soon got over being surprised,' said Tamsyn softly. 'I expect they had a lovely wedding, and lived happily ever after.' And then she added anxiously, 'I do hope they were always very careful about leaving cream outside the back door for the Fairy Folk, and not picking rampion at Midsummer, and things like that. They—they'd sort of have to be more careful than most, wouldn't they?'

Aunt Deborah laughed her soft, warm laugh. 'I'm sure they were very careful,' she said. 'And now—as soon as Giles has done stuffing himself with chestnuts, it is time you all three went to bed.'

So Giles swallowed the last crumbs of hot chestnut in a hurry, and turned very red in the face and watery about the eyes because they were very hot indeed; Tamsyn put away the partlet strip in the carved chest where she and Beatrix and Aunt Deborah all kept their sewing; and the three of them took their chamber candles and said goodnight, and made their bow and dropped their curtsies. Then they all trooped upstairs, Giles to the little garret under the eaves that he shared with Piers, and Beatrix and Tamsyn to their own chamber, where Littlest had already been asleep for hours in his little truckle-bed under the window, with Lammy clutched to his chest.

8 *Uncle Martin Comes for Christmas*

A little before Christmas a most lovely thing happened. Aunt Deborah had a letter from Uncle Martin. It came all the way from Bideford in a coasting vessel, and the sailor to whom Uncle Martin had given it brought it up from Billingsgate one morning, on his way home to his family in St. Albans.

The letter said that Uncle Martin was coming up to London on business, and to spend Christmas with his brother and sister-in-law, and would be arriving, roads, weather and footpads permitting, on Thursday next. (In those days people didn't generally ask if they could come to visit you, because it took so long to get an answer; they just wrote to say they were coming, and came. Sometimes they just came, without writing first of all.)

Aunt Deborah read the letter while the family watched her breathlessly; and then she told them that Uncle Martin was coming to stay for Christmas. The Almost-Twins and Littlest were very noisy with excitement, because they had never seen Uncle Martin, and an unknown Uncle coming to stay is an exciting sort of thing. But Tamsyn just said, 'Oh-h!' very softly, and turned bright pink under her brown, and didn't say any more at all, because it was so lovely that just at first she couldn't quite believe it, and when she got to believing it, she didn't want to talk about it to anyone, except perhaps to Piers, and Piers was at work.

Then Aunt Deborah gave the sailor cold beef and brown bread and cider in the kitchen, because he said, Yes, he was rather hungry, when she asked him. And Tamsyn slipped down after them and sat on the salt-butter cask and watched him with shining eyes while he ate and drank. Beatrix had not come down to the kitchen, because she said the sailor was dirty, and Giles had had to set off for school, and Meg was busy making pastry at the other end of the kitchen table; and so Tamsyn was left in peace to sit on the salt-butter cask by her lone, and feel very, very happy, and gaze at the sailor. She thought he was quite the nicest-looking sailor that she had ever seen. He had a ruddy face rather spoilt by rough weather, and little, bright, grey eyes with wrinkles all round them that had come from so much screwing them up to look into the distance. He had gold rings in his ears, and a curly, quirky mouth that stretched right across his face, and clothes that were salt-stained and sun-faded and so ragged that the brown skin of his arms and shoulders showed through. And besides all this, he had brought the wonderful letter from Uncle Martin.

At first the sailor was too busy eating to talk much, but every now and then he winked at Tamsyn or Meg the Kitchen, by way of politeness; and after a time he began to eat more slowly, as though he was beginning to be full. So Tamsyn thought perhaps he could spare a little time for talking now, and she leaned forward on the salt-butter cask and said would he please tell her about where he had been and the adventures that he had had.

The sailor seemed only too pleased; and between mouthfuls of beef and draughts of cider, he told her how he had sailed all the seas that there were to sail, and served under Sebastian Cabot, in the *Mathew* of Bristol town, when he discovered the West Indies, and how he had seen the glories of the New World, and talked with men who had mouths and eyes in their chests and no heads at all, and how he had almost discovered the North-West Passage to Cathay. He talked on and on, while Meg the Kitchen (who was not nearly so deaf when she wanted to hear something) stared at him open-mouthed between every roll of the rolling-pin, and Tamsyn leaned so far forward on the salt-butter cask that she came very near to losing her balance, because it was so tremendously exciting to meet someone who really *had* been to the New World and seen the things that she and Piers so desperately longed to see.

'Ah well,' said the sailor at last, finishing up the cider and pushing away his empty plate, 'the sea is a good place, and the land is a good place too, and just now 'tis the land as calls Jabez Varley—for Jabez Varley be my baptismal name, little Mistress. 'Tis two years since I seed my wife and childer; and now I'm off home to spend Christmas with them, and the sea behind me and the good smells of the earth to welcome me back; for I was farm-bred. And maybe I'll stay at home a year and help wi' the harvest, and maybe I'll not; and if I'd any sense I'd stay home for good, but well I knows that when the sap rises in the spring the old unrest'll wake in Jabez Varley's blood, and I'll turn my face to the sea again, hungry for the cold salt smell of it as I am this morning for the smell of fresh ploughed earth.'

Then Aunt Deborah came down again, and gave the sailor a mutton pasty and a silver piece to help him on his way; for it was a long way to St. Albans. And he put on his ragged seaman's bonnet so that he could doff it to her, and gave Tamsyn one last enormous wink, and went off blithely, to be home in time for Christmas and make merry with his family, and work on an inland farm until the sea called him back again.

Then there began to be a great hustling and bustling, because of getting ready for Uncle Martin as well as getting ready for Christmas. Tamsyn helped Aunt Deborah and Meg the Kitchen to make the guest-room ready. They spread clean, lavender-scented linen on the bed, and shook out the embroidered crimson bed-curtains, in case there should be any spiders in the corners. They spread fresh rushes and rosemary and hyssop on the floor, and put a little posy of sweet-smelling herbs in a yellow pottery jar on the big clothes-chest, to make the room smell nice. When the guest-chamber was as ready as ready could be, with honey-wax candles on the side chest and the very best linen head-sheet covering the goose-down pillows, they shut the door on it carefully, to keep the cleanness and tidiness in and Littlest out. Then they went on with the baking and brewing and stoning raisins and crushing sugar-candy, and polishing the best pewter, and washing Aunt Deborah's treasured Venetian goblets (but of course nobody was allowed to touch those, except Aunt Deborah herself; they were much too precious). And every time Tamsyn passed the door of the guest-room, she couldn't help opening it just a little way and peeping inside, because seeing the room all fresh and ready for its guest helped her to believe that it was not all a dream, and that Uncle Martin would really and truly soon be here.

It was four whole days between the coming of the sailor with the letter and the arrival of Uncle Martin, and it seemed to Tamsyn that they would never go. But Sunday went by somehow, and then Monday, and then Tuesday; and then it was Wednesday, and Uncle Martin would be coming tomorrow! Tamsyn added up every one of her sums wrong on Wednesday morning, and made every one of the cross-stitches in a whole pansy-head in her sampler facing the wrong way, so that she had to unpick them all again.

Then at last it was Thursday! Time for lessons, and Tamsyn made the most dreadful mess of her copy. Time to go out shopping, and her inside swayed gently up and down and gave queer little jumps all the while they were out, in case Uncle Martin should have travelled quicker than they expected, and be there when they got back; but of course he hadn't and he wasn't! Time for dinner, and Tamsyn was much too excited to eat, though she did try, because it was a very nice dinner. Slowly the winter's afternoon wore away, with Tamsyn and Beatrix rushing from the kitchen, where they were helping Meg to make frumenty, every time a horse came along the street. Just at twilight Giles came home, whooping up the street because there was no more school for twelve whole days, and Christmas just ahead and an exciting unknown uncle coming to spend it with them. But still there was no sign of Uncle Martin.

'He wouldn't be here yet, lovey—not unless he rode very fast indeed on the last stage,' said Aunt Deborah, comfortingly, to Tamsyn, as they all trooped upstairs to the parlour. 'And he'll have to leave the horse at the inn, too, before he comes on to us.'

In the warm parlour the others gathered round the fire to eat their afternoon bread and raisins, but Tamsyn took hers away by herself to the deep bay window that overhung the street, and curled up on the cushioned sill with her nose pressed against the panes. It was beginning to be quite dusk, and she could see the candles behind her reflected in the glass, like tiny golden crocuses dancing there, and little broken reflections of Aunt Deborah in her great chair, and the Almost-Twins and Littlest and Lammy and Bunch all mixed up together round her feet, but not Piers nor Uncle Gideon, because they were still at work—she could hear the ring of the hand-hammer and the deep roar of the forge coming up from the workshop below. The tulip was reflected in the window too. It was still tight shut, but the bud was fat and big and red as Christmas holly, and the edges of the petals were just beginning to curl back. It would certainly be open by Christmas Eve—a flower like a scarlet lamp, just the shape of the great stern-lanterns she had seen high up on the poops of the tall ships of Bideford Town. Lovely! Tamsyn poked it very gently with the tip of her right forefinger. Then she looked into the street again. Everything beyond the reflected candle-flames was blue in the dusk, a lovely soft blue that looked as though you could stroke it, and all down the street windows were lighting up, yellow as wild wallflowers. If she looked straight downwards she could see the light that streamed out from the workshop window making a golden patch on the cobbles; there were golden patches under every lighted window in the street, and Tamsyn noticed that there was beginning to be a sort of pale look to the ground and faint, white blurs on window-sills and in the angles of gables. And when she looked up at the candle-lit window of Master Bodkin-the-Goldsmith's house over the way, there were little whirling flakes drifting down between her and it. Snow!

Tamsyn didn't say anything about the snow, because she knew that if she did, the Almost-Twins would come rushing over to look, and she wanted her window-sill and the scarlet tulip all to herself. But she didn't have it like that very long, because as soon as Littlest had finished his bread and raisins and wiped some of the stickiness off on Bunch, he came trundling over to join her. Still, she didn't mind Littlest, any more than she would have minded Piers. She liked Littlest and Piers best of all the Dolphin House family.

'Tamsyn,' said Littlest firmly, 'help Littlest up,' and he began to scramble up on to the window-sill.

Tamsyn put her arms round his middle and heaved him up beside her. 'Upsy-daisy.'

'Littlest *loves* you,' said Littlest, staggering to his feet on the cushions and holding on to her face to keep himself steady.

Tamsyn hugged him close, feeling all warm inside because he was such a dear little boy. '*Do* you, Littlest?' she whispered.

'Yiss,' said Littlest. And then he saw the whiteness outside. 'Snow!' he shouted, very pleased with himself for having remembered since last year. 'Snow! Snow! Snow in dis street! Littlest *likes* snow.' And he began to jig up and down, holding on to Tamsyn's face with one hand and beating Lammy's tin legs against the window with the other, because of being so pleased.

Then of course the Almost-Twins came rushing from the fire and flung themselves against the window to look, breathing all over the panes so that the little, dancing candle-flames were blotted out, and shouting and exclaiming and making a great deal of noise. And in the middle of it all there came a bobbing torch down below, and a knocking at the workshop door—and Uncle Martin had arrived!

The Almost-Twins made a rush towards the stairs, but somehow Tamsyn got there before them, even though she *had* remembered to lift Littlest down from the window-sill first. She kilted up her brown skirts and went whirling down and down and round and round, calling as she ran, 'Uncle Martin! Uncle Martin! It's *me*! I'm coming! It's *me*, Uncle Martin!'

The workshop was full of the leaping red light of the forge fire, so that it glowed like the heart of a ruby; and the street door was open, and there, with the whirling snow-storm behind him, was Uncle Martin, square and blithe and ruddy, beating the snow from his bonnet, and Uncle Gideon, still in his leather apron, striding to meet him with hand outstretched. But Tamsyn got there first! With one final squeal of 'It's *me*, Uncle Martin!' she flew straight into his arms, and Uncle Martin caught her up and hugged her as though he never meant to leave off.

'Tamsy!' said Uncle Martin. 'Why, Tamsy, my honey, how you've grown!'

And Tamsyn drove her nose harder and harder into his chest, and dragged him down and clung round his neck, and all she could say, and she couldn't say that very clearly, because of her nose being so squashed, was just 'Uncle Bartid! Uncle *Bartid*!' over and over again. At last Uncle Martin stopped hugging her, and shook hands with Uncle Gideon, and the Almost-Twins came clamouring round him, quite forgetting their bow and curtsy in their excitement, and Piers left the bellows to Timothy and came over in his quiet way to wring Uncle Martin's hand, and Uncle Martin was trying to greet everybody and pay the boy who had guided him from the inn at the same time. Then Aunt Deborah came rustling downstairs with her wide skirts gathered in one hand and Littlest's sticky paw in the other, looking perfectly lovely and quite unruffled by all the noise and excitement, to tell Uncle Martin how glad they were to see him. 'Though indeed, I do not think you can doubt that,' said she, smiling at him, as Littlest added his own voice to the uproar.

'My Uncle Martin!' said Littlest loudly, 'I've got my new shoes on—look!' and he stuck out one fat foot in a little square-toed crimson shoe, to prove it.

'Vain little poppet!' said his mother; and then she looked at Uncle Martin again, and said, 'Come your ways upstairs; you must be tired and hungry, and supper will soon be ready.'

So Piers picked up Uncle Martin's saddle-bags, and they all went upstairs again somehow, with Tamsyn clinging to Uncle Martin's hand. And presently they sat down to supper, even Littlest, who was being allowed to stay up late for the very first time, in honour of the occasion.

It was very hard to keep the Silence at Meals rule that evening, especially for Tamsyn, because there were so many things bubbling inside her that she wanted to say to Uncle Martin. But supper was an extra-specially nice one, with pink marchpane and sticky dried fruit and roast goose and things like that; and that helped a lot, especially as Tamsyn was very hungry after not having had much dinner; because if you are busy enough eating, you haven't really time to talk much, however badly you want to. So she sat as quiet as a mouse, eating everything that came her way, and smiling blithely at Uncle Martin across the glimmering candle-flames, with a lovely warm feeling of happiness inside her.

Presently supper was over and Silence at Meals was over too, and Meg the Kitchen cleared away the dishes, and Aunt Deborah came back from putting a very sleepy Littlest to bed; and everybody gathered round the fire of pine logs. (You couldn't burn coal in London while Parliament was sitting, in case the smoke might be bad for the Members.) The grown-ups sat in their great upright chairs, and the children squatted on their heels among the warm rushes, and Bunch sprawled with his front to the blaze, fluttering his paws and twitching his ears as he chased dream rabbits. Tamsyn sat between Piers and Uncle Martin, blinking at the fire like a baby owl, and feeling very happy, and very full, and a little sleepy, and rubbed her cheek against Uncle Martin's knee until he began to tickle the back of her neck, just as he used to do in the old days before she left Bideford and came to live in the Dolphin House. At first everybody talked a lot, Tamsyn too; but after a time it was just the grown-ups who talked, and talked, and talked;

and Tamsyn got more and more sleepy, and blinked faster and faster at the dancing flames, until she really did look just like a baby owl with soft, fluffed-out feathers and bright, blinky eyes. Everything seemed blurred into a golden mist that was made of happiness and sleepiness and firelight all mixed up together; and presently, out of the mist she heard Uncle Martin talking about the *Joyous Venture*, how she would be launched in a month's time and sailing for the West Indies on her maiden voyage in the spring; and the trade with the New World, which would be a very great trade one day, and about how the *Joyous Venture* would be able to outsail any ship of the West Country, because she was to carry topgallant sails like the *Great Harry*, the King's Flagship. Oh, she would be beautiful! Swift and beautiful, sailing wide-winged into the Golden West. . . .

Aunt Deborah said suddenly, 'Bedtime, poppets, and here's Tamsyn half asleep as she sits! Run along now, my dears.'

So they collected their candles and made their bows and their curtsies, and went trooping upstairs, shivering and squeaking because it was so very cold in the bedrooms. Long after Beatrix was asleep Tamsyn lay rubbing her cold feet together to warm them, staring at the queer snow-light on the ceiling through a gap in the bed curtains, and listening to Uncle Martin's voice in the parlour below and the whisper of the falling snow beyond the window. But at last she fell asleep, and dreamed that she and Piers and the red tulip were all three sailing into the west, through sapphire seas frilled with white waves and trimmed with dear little leaping dolphins.

For two days Uncle Martin was out most of the time about the business that had brought him to London Town; and generally Uncle Gideon or Piers or Timothy went with him to show him the way to wherever he wanted to go, because he had only been to London once before, and that was nearly twenty years ago, when he came to see Uncle Gideon and Aunt Deborah married, and so he did not remember his way about very well.

Then on the third evening, while they were all sitting round the fire after supper, Meg the Kitchen came stumping upstairs with a note for Uncle Martin, and said that a seaman had brought it and gone away again because there was no reply.

'Ah, from John Bourdekin,' said Uncle Martin, beginning to read the note. 'You remember him, Gideon? He was apprenticed in Braund's shipyard along East-the-Water when we were little lads.'

'Yes, I do remember him, though I'd not given him a thought for twenty years.'

'Then you don't know that he has risen to be Master Shipwright at Deptford Royal Dockyard?' asked Uncle Martin, with his funny red eyebrows shooting up towards his hair.

Uncle Gideon shook his head and said that he certainly did not, and that he supposed Uncle Martin was going to see him.

'Why, yes,' said Uncle Martin. 'I liked John Bourdekin in the old days, and I've always had a mind to see round a Royal Dockyard. I sent word to him yesterday that I was in London, and meant to visit him, and this is his reply, bidding me go down tomorrow. Will you ride with me?'

Uncle Gideon shook his head again. 'No, no, Martin old lad, I hardly knew him.'

'Will you lend me Piers, then, to show me the way?' asked Uncle Martin.

Uncle Gideon looked at Piers doubtfully, and said, 'I should not think he knows it himself.'

But Piers said, 'I do, sir! I know it quite well!' in a voice that cracked with eagerness.

So it was arranged that Piers was to ride down to Deptford with his Uncle next day, and oh! Tamsyn did so wish she were going too. She wished it so desperately that her wishing showed all over her face, and Uncle Martin looked at her very hard for a moment, and said, 'Do you want to come very badly, honey?'

Tamsyn wanted to come so badly that she couldn't speak a word; but she nodded, with her eyes fixed beseechingly on Uncle Martin's face and her hands screwed together in her lap.

Now of course it wouldn't have been fair for Uncle Martin to have taken Tamsyn and not the others, but Beatrix didn't care much for ships and was afraid of getting dirty or falling down holes, and Giles was going to play football with some friends, and neither of them wanted to come, so after a little discussion Uncle Martin asked Aunt Deborah if she would lend him Tamsyn for the day.

'But Mistress Bourdekin won't want a strange little girl to spend the day,' protested Aunt Deborah, laughing. 'It's different about Piers, because he's going to show you the way—at least I hope he is; but there's no *excuse* for Tamsyn to go. You can't just take people to spend the day with perfect strangers who haven't invited them—really you can't!'

'I can,' said Uncle Martin, quite simply, and his eyes began to dance. 'But if 'twill set your mind at rest, I *did* mention in my letter that I should probably bring a couple of my kinsfolk with me.'

'Well,' said Aunt Deborah, and she looked from Uncle Martin's dancing eyes to Piers' eager face and Tamsyn's beseeching one. And she said, 'Very well, you shall have her, Martin; but please don't let her fall into a dry dock if you can help it.'

And Tamsyn jumped up and flung her arms round Aunt Deborah's neck and hugged her.

9 *Down to Deptford*

So next morning Tamsyn put on her second-best russet-brown kirtle
—not her best kirtle, because you cannot really enjoy yourself much in
a dockyard in your best kirtle, and not her everyday kirtle,
because you cannot very well go visiting in your everyday kirtle,
even if the neat patch on the skirt where you tore it on a nail *does*
hardly show. Then Aunt Deborah muffled her close in her warm
frieze cloak of kingfisher blue with the orange-tawny lining to the
hood. And she was waiting on the doorstep with Uncle Martin a
good ten minutes before Piers rode up on one of the horses that
had been ordered from the Fountain Tavern, leading the other
horse behind him.

Uncle Martin swung into the saddle, and Uncle Gideon lifted
Tamsyn up to the pillion. The horse was a very tall one, and the
ground seemed a very long way away, but that only made it all seem
even more exciting.

'Hold tight, my honey,' said Uncle Martin; and Tamsyn twisted her
hands in his belt and said she was, and they were off!

Along the crowded streets they went at a trot, and then they
swung right and clattered across London Bridge. It was bitterly
cold, with a little icy wind and a sky the colour of grey sheep's wool
that seemed almost to touch the pointed gables of the houses, and the
hurrying crowds blew on their fingers and had very red noses, but they
all had on their brightest clothes and they all seemed very happy, for
tomorrow was Christmas Eve.

The three-day-old snow had been churned to a brown slush under-
foot, but along every wall-top and window-ledge and gable-corner it
was clean and crisp and white, as though it had just that minute
fallen; and when they reached the Southwark shore, and Tamsyn
looked up at the spire of St. Mary of the Ferry as they rode by,
she saw that every ledge and cranny and fretted pinnacle carried
its load of frozen snow.

Southwark was even more crowded and noisy and cheerful than the
City had been, but then it always was, because all the strolling

players and pick-pockets and dancing bears who weren't wanted in London were ferried across to Southwark by order of the Mayor and Aldermen and left there. Even the roofs had a rakish sort of look, and the clothes of the people were extra-specially bright, as though to make up for some of them being extra-specially ragged. There were fights going on at street corners, and a wandering fiddler playing a jig in the gutter with a little dog in a red jacket dancing for pennies.

On rode the three, threading their way through the busy crowds, past the Tabard Inn, and took the Canterbury Road. Soon the crowds grew thinner and the houses were left behind, and they were out in the open country; and the road led away and away between whitened fields, beckoning them down to Deptford, where the great ships were lying. High in the bare, lacy tops of the elm trees last year's rooks' nests swayed against the grey sheep's-wool sky, and the wind that swayed them smelt cold, tingling, raw, exciting cold; it smelt of snow.

Tamsyn sniffed hard, and it did smell of snow.

'There's more snow coming,' said Piers, sniffing too.

'Ah well, as long as it doesn't come on before we get back tonight,' said Uncle Martin.

'More snow for Christmas,' said Tamsyn blithely. 'How nice!'

Round the next bend of the way they passed a countryman bringing in a great bale of scarlet-berried holly to market, and exchanged Merry Christmases with him, and soon after that the road branched and they headed down towards Deptford.

Then the little cold wind began to smell quite different. It still smelt of snow, but it smelt of other things too—exciting things: salt and pitch, rope and timber and wood smoke. And quite suddenly, over the brow of a hill and round the corner of the road, there was Deptford! A huddle of grey and russet roofs and the river beyond, and the bare woods beyond again; and between the town and the river was the Royal Dockyard, and the tapering masts of the King's ships rising above the roofs of the houses.

'Look!' cried Tamsyn. 'There are *ships*!'

'Why, honey, there generally are, in a dockyard,' said Uncle Martin, laughing.

Piers didn't say anything, but Tamsyn knew that he understood, and that he felt just the same as she did about those tall ships.

They rode down into the narrow streets beside the Dockyard, and the smell grew stronger and more breathtakingly exciting, and every other house seemed to be a ship's chandler's or an instrument maker's. The crowds were mostly sailors in salt-stained clothes with gold rings in their ears, and at the end of every alley-way was the grey shimmer of the river and the white wings of the wheeling gulls.

After asking their way once or twice they found the Master Ship-wright's house in a narrow court close to the Dockyard wall. It seemed very quiet there after the busy streets, for the houses round it all belonged to important Dockyard folk, and it did not lead anywhere, and so there was no coming and going in it at all. It was a nice court; the houses had each a little strip of garden before them where blue-green snowdrops snouts were already poking up through the snow-speckled earth, and high above the russet roofs at the far end rose the masts of a tall ship.

What a lovely place to live, thought Tamsyn, so close to the great Yard, with the fine men-of-war coming and going, and always new ships being built and launched and sailing away down to the sea, and other new ships taking their places.

Mistress Bourdekin was standing in her doorway as they reined up. She was as tiny and brown and shrivelled as a winter leaf, and her eyes were as bright as a robin's, and her gown and kirtle as gay as holly-berries. 'Here you are!' she cried, darting out to greet them. 'I heard the horses and I knew it must be you—and the little maid too! Poor chick, she must be shrammed with the cold. Come your ways in, good people, come in out of the cold, all of you this moment! Peter will take the horses up to the stable. Peter! Pe-ter! Where has that boy got to? *Peter!*'

A gardener-groom sort of person with a broad, cheerful grin appeared suddenly behind her, and went to the horses's heads. Piers doffed his bonnet and swung down from his saddle and lifted Tamsyn down too, and Uncle Martin dismounted likewise. Peter and the horses disappeared up the court, and Mistress Bourdekin hustled everybody indoors, chattering all the time so hard that nobody, not even Uncle Martin, could get a word in edgeways. She took off Tamsyn's cloak, and shooed them, as though they were chickens, into a long, lovely room, where the table was already spread with white damask and bright pewter, and a fire of sea-coal blazed on the hearth, and the panelled walls were decked with holly and ivy in honour of Christmas. Then she stopped and looked at them with her head on one side like a robin.

'My good man is down at the Yard,' she said, 'but he'll be home any moment now, and then he'll be free for all the afternoon. *You* will be Master Martin Caunter. We have never met before, but of course I know you must be because one of you *has* to be, and it couldn't very well be either of the other two, could it?'

Uncle Martin bowed very gravely, though his eyes twinkled. 'You are quite correct, Mistress Bourdekin; I *am* Martin Caunter,' he said; and he presented and explained Piers and Tamsyn.

Piers bowed, and Tamsyn spread her russet skirts and dropped her best curtsy; and Mistress Bourdekin returned the bow and curtsy with a crinkly smile, and said, 'Come to the fire now, do, for 'tis cold enough to freeze your toes and fingers off, and you'll have a cold afternoon, my poor chicks.'

So they all crowded round the fire, and Tamsyn squatted down on her cold heels and held out her cold hands to the blaze, and Piers squatted down beside her, and held out his hands, too.

'Glory! Doesn't the fire feel good,' said Piers.

'Mmm!' said Tamsyn.'Oh, isn't this loverly.'

And Piers looked down at her in his funny quiet way, but he didn't say any more.

At that moment Master Bourdekin came home for his dinner. He was as big and burly as Mistress Bourdekin was small and shrivelled, with a great hooked nose and a golden beard streaked with silver, looking a little like a Viking, but pinker and not so fierce. And after Uncle Martin and he had wrung each other by the hand and clapped each other on the shoulder a great many times, Piers and Tamsyn were explained and presented again, and made another bow and another curtsy. Then a pair of larded capons and a beautiful raised-pie steaming through a hole in its golden-brown pastry lid were brought in and set on the side-chest, and everybody gathered to their dinner. But before they sat down, Master Bourdekin said Grace. At least, it was not Grace exactly. 'For all who go down to the sea in ships and occupy their business in great waters, that we on the land may sleep secure and eat when we are hungry, the Lord make us truly thankful,' said Master Bourdekin.

The raised pie was as good as it looked, for it was full of ham and eggs and pigeons and spice, all swimming in thick brown gravy that you had to sop up with crusty bread; and it was so hot and spicy and delicious that it seemed to go right down through Tamsyn until it reached her cold toes and made them all tingly warm again. Uncle Martin and Master Bourdekin talked about old times and new trade and ship-building, with their elbows on the table; and Piers sat listening to every word they said and almost forgetting to eat his dinner, although he was quite as hungry as Tamsyn; and Mistress Bourdekin chatted away to Tamsyn about Christmas when *she* was a little girl. And Tamsyn ate solidly, and listened to Mistress Bourdekin with one ear, and to Master Bourdekin and Uncle Martin with the other; so she was kept really very busy all through dinner.

'Topgallant sails,' Uncle Martin was saying, 'and a laced bonnet to the mainsail. She'll outsail any ship of the West Country.'

'Topgallant sails, hey?' Master Bourdekin replied, with a kindling eye. 'In a hundred years from now there'll not be a ship built that doesn't carry topgallant sails; but today . . .'

'When I was a little girl, good St. Nicholas used to leave a gilded walnut and a sugar-top in the toes of the pair of shoes I put out for him,' said Mistress Bourdekin. 'Always the walnut in the *right* toe, and the sugar-top in the *left,* and then the other things on top. One Christmas he brought me a doll with gold spangles on her kirtle and the most beautiful pink cheeks, and I loved her dearly, but my brothers dropped her down the well, playing at ducking witches, and though we fished and *fished* with a bent pin, we never got her out again.'

After the raised pie and larded capons there was a great cake of gingerbread and queer, sweet, dried fruit in syrup; and after that Tamsyn was quite full. But Master Bourdekin and Uncle Martin were still drawing trade routes and designs of ships on the table-cloth with their fingers, and Piers was still listening with his chin in his hands and his eyes all bright and far-off looking.

So Mistress Bourdekin rose and shook out her skirts and smiled at Tamsyn. 'Let you and me go back to the fire until the menfolk have finished playing,' she said.

So they went back to the fire; and Tamsyn sat down on her heels, and they looked at each other. Mistress Bourdekin was not the least bit pretty, like Aunt Deborah, but her eyes were very merry, and her face changed all the time as quickly as the thoughts changed inside her head, so that it seemed to shimmer, and Tamsyn liked her tremendously. They talked about all sorts of things: about Christmas and ships and gingerbread and gardens; and Mistress Bourdekin told Tamsyn about her two sons who were grown up now and away at sea, but had done the most *dreadful* things when they were little, like setting fire to the apple-loft with themselves inside it, and pretending to be sickening for the smallpox when Cardinal Wolsey came to see the Dockyard, and frightening the poor man into fits lest he should catch it, because he had been rude about their dog. And Tamsyn told Mistress Bourdekin about Bideford and about her red tulip that was almost open, and about the time that Littlest grew a peacock's tail.

At last the menfolk pushed back their chairs and got up.

'Now we had best be getting down to the Yard,' said Master Bourdekin. 'These winter afternoons close in so early, and there is a goodish lot to be seen.'

So they all trooped back into the hall, and Mistress Bourdekin bundled Tamsyn up in the blue cloak with the orange-tawny lining, and then they all set off; and Mistress Bourdekin went in again and shut the door, for she was not coming with them. She could see the Dockyard any day she liked, and she was used to it.

Master Bourdekin and Uncle Martin went first, still talking hard, and Piers dropped behind and took Tamsyn's hand. They didn't talk at all, because Piers seldom talked much anyway, and Tamsyn was feeling too excited inside; she was so excited inside that she gave a little hop every three steps. Excitement, and happiness, and magic, and things like that always went to Tamsyn's toes, and made her hop. They turned left at the opening of the court, and there, right in front of them, was a gate in a high wall; a broad gate, big enough to let through the great wains that brought timber down from the forests to build the King's ships; and they went through, and then they were really and truly in Deptford Royal Dockyard!

'Oh!' said Tamsyn. 'O-oh!' and then she didn't say any more. The Royal Dockyard seemed very big, even bigger than the shipyards at Bideford, and from end to end and from wall to river, it was full of a great coming and going of seamen who sailed the ships and shipwrights and caulkers and smiths who built them; the clatter and ring of hammers on anvils and the rasp of saws sawing great oak trunks into ships' timbers, and the mingled smell of rope and pitch and salt and woodsmoke was stronger than ever. There were huge sheds with narrow, white drifts of snow still lying against their walls, and a red line of bonfires burning rubbish, and high above the roofs of the sheds rose the tall masts of the King's ships, towering into the sky.

That was a very wonderful afternoon! Holding tight to Piers' hand and occasionally treading on Master Bourdekin's heels in her eagerness, Tamsyn explored sail-lofts and rigging-lofts and rope-walks. She saw the huge kilns where the timbers were boiled until the shipwrights could bend them to the curve of the ships' sides; and the sheds where the tree-trunks were stacked to season for a year (for Master Bourdekin said that oak was not good for shipbuilding until a year after it had been cut). She saw great masts and spars being built of fir wood clamped together by iron rings, and the Dockyard sheer-legs, which was a thing for stepping the masts into ships after they had been launched. She saw a long shed called a mould-loft, that seemed as big as a cathedral, where Master Boudekin designed every ship that was built in the Dockyard, drawing her deck-plan full size on the floor, very much as Piers had drawn the *Dolphin and Joyous Venture* on the floor of Kit's Castle, and her side view and her stern view, from keel to poop-rail on the towering white-washed walls, so that the shipwrights under him could see the exact size and shape of every plank and timber. There was a great ship drawn out there now, and after they had looked at the drawings on the floor and walls, Master Bourdekin took them to see the ship herself. She was in a dry dock that had a thing rather like a mill-wheel at one end to bale out the water, for she was going to be a very big ship, five hundred tons burthen, Master Bourdekin said, and most of the big ships of King Henry's Navy were built in dry docks. She was only a keel of elm timbers, and bare ribs of seasoned oak, yet awhile, but one day she would be a tall and stately man-of-war, with gold-work on her prow and stern, and guns between her decks to protect the new trade of England.

But not all the ships in Deptford Dockyard were unfinished ones; there were others which had sailed the seas for years, and come home to be refitted or simply because they were not needed just now, and were made fast to the quays and jetties with what Master Bourdekin called a care and maintenance crew on board. And among these was the *Mary Rose* herself; the incomparable *Mary Rose,* which could outsail every ship of the King's Fleet—even the *Great Harry.* And oh, she was lovely, resting like a swan on the grey water that caught the wintry light in its ripples and made shimmering criss-cross light-patterns along her sides. All her gilding was as joyous as marigolds on her proud stern and forecastle, for she had been newly gilded in readiness for the spring review, and her bare masts and spars loomed dark against the grey sheep's-wool sky.

Master Bourdekin had not told them that the *Mary Rose* was in the Dockyard; he had kept it as a surprise, so that he could enjoy their astonished faces when they saw how superbly beautiful she was; and when he spoke of her he did it in the sort of voice that some-one might use in speaking of their Queen. For Master Bourdekin had built the *Mary Rose,* and he loved her the best of all his ships.

But the ship that seemed loveliest of all to Tamsyn, and to Piers too, was quite a little one; and she was not even finished yet, but lay in the slips that sloped down to the water, with workmen swarming all round her. And she was so beautiful that Tamsyn's heart went out to her the moment she saw her, and she could not say a single word, but just stood and gazed and gazed, while Uncle Martin and Master Bourdekin talked to the workmen.

Presently Uncle Martin asked when the ship would be ready for launching.

'In about a month's time,' said Master Bourdekin. 'But by the time she has her masts stepped and her rigging complete, she'll not be ready to sail before the spring.'

Then he and Uncle Martin moved away to speak to a foreman; but Piers and Tamsyn stood quite still where they were, gazing up at the lovely ship, with all the bustle and noise of the Dockyard quite forgotten, so that it was just the three of them, Piers and Tamsyn and the ship, alone to themselves in all the world. There she lay, disdainful of the comings and goings all around her, her castles lifting above the slipway, and her bowsprit reaching out towards the open water, as though she was growing eager for the sea-ways in her sleep. For Tamsyn was sure that she was asleep, like the bare woods across the river; and in the first days of the spring she and the woods would awake, and the sap would rise in the trees and the buds begin to thicken, and the sails would break out from the bare masts of the ship, and she would sail away. She was lovely now, in her winter sleep, so lovely that it hurt deep down inside you to look at her, but she would be a hundred times lovelier when the spring came. Tamsyn knew the ways of ships, she had seen them so often at home before she came to live in London, and she knew how this ship would rise and curtsy to the seas, and how her sails would fill and she would heel over gently into the wind, as she sped down river and away across the world.

'Oh, Piers!' she whispered at last. 'She's like the *Dolphin and Joyous Venture*.'

And Piers said in a queer, hushed sort of voice, 'I'd give all the world to be aboard when she sails, and feel her lift as the sea takes her.'

Then Uncle Martin and Master Bourdekin came back; and Uncle Martin put a hand on Piers' shoulder, and said, 'Isn't she a beauty?'

'Yes, Uncle Martin,' said Piers.

And Master Bourdekin stopped looking at the ship, and looked hard at Piers instead. 'You are not going to sea, hey?' he asked in an abrupt sort of way.

Piers' nose went white under his freckles, and he said, 'No, sir; I'm apprenticed to my father—he's a swordsmith.'

'A pity,' said Master Bourdekin. 'You are a likely looking lad, and you have the love of ships and the sea in you. And there's never been a time like this for English seamen.'

Piers said, 'I know, sir,' rather quickly.

And Master Bourdekin looked at him harder than ever, pulling gently at his golden beard, and demanded, 'Then *why* aren't you going to sea?'

'My eldest brother was drowned two years ago, and of course I have to take his place and follow my father's trade,' Piers told him.

Master Bourdekin went on pulling his beard. 'Ah,' he said, 'I suppose there is no help for it, then; but 'tis a pity, a great pity.'

But Uncle Martin was a hopeful person, and he protested. 'Don't croak, John. Nothing is ever certain in this world, and the bad things least of all.' Then he gave Piers' shoulder a little shake. 'Never you forget that, my lad, and never you forget that there's a place for you aboard one of my ships, if ever the day comes when you can take it.'

'It's—it's very good of you, sir,' said Piers. 'I'll not forget.'

But Tamsyn knew that he didn't believe for an instant that that day would ever come.

It was time for them to be getting back, for already the light was beginning to fade and the milky sparkle was gone from the river. So after one last look at the ship that was so like the *Dolphin and Joyous Venture*, they turned back the way they had come. Tamsyn and Piers still walked hand in hand behind the other two, and

Tamsyn looked back regretfully many times before the lovely ship was hidden by sheds and lofts; but Piers never looked back at all.

When they got to the Master Shipwright's house again they found the candles were already lit, and Mistress Bourdekin hustled them all into the warm room where the holly sparkled on the walls and the fire blazed half up the chimney, to toast themselves and eat sugar-bread and dried apricots while the horses were brought round. She wanted them to stay to supper, but of course they couldn't do that because of the long ride home.

Then they heard Peter bring the horses round, and they all trooped outside again, and Mistress Bourdekin bundled Tamsyn up in her cloak once more, and kissed her on the top of her head. (She didn't usually like being kissed, but she didn't mind Mistress Bourdekin.) There were good-byes and hand-clasps and bows and curtsies and Thank-you-very-much-for-having-me's; and Uncle Martin mounted his horse and Piers lifted Tamsyn up behind him and then swung into his own saddle; and then Uncle Martin was leaning down to shake hands with Master Bourdekin once more, and Mistress Bourdekin, who had been standing in her lighted doorway, kilted up her skirts and came darting out again to whisper to Tamsyn, 'Come and see me again one day, sweetheart.'

'I will,' said Tamsyn, leaning down as far as she dared, from the high pillion saddle. 'Oh, I *will*!'

Then they really were off, leaving the Master Shipwright and Mistress Bourdekin waving after them in the yellow light that streamed out from the open doorway across the snow.

'Good-bye,' called Piers and Tamsyn and Uncle Martin. 'A Merry Christmas to you!'

And, 'A Merry Christmas! Good-bye! Good-bye!' called back Master Bourdekin and his wife, until they were round the corner and clattering up the street towards open country.

It had grown quite dark while they were in Mistress Bourdekin's candle-lit parlour; and when they were clear of the town, and Tamsyn turned to look back, the lights of Deptford shone golden among the snowy fields, and beyond them the riding-lights of the ships sparkled against the furry darkness of the woods across the river.

It seemed a very long way home, but it was not nearly so cold as it had been when they rode out in the morning; and suddenly, just short of Southwark, Tamsyn felt something like a tiny ice-cold feather settle on the tip of her nose.

'Here's the snow!' she cried.

So they rode through Southwark with the first flakes of the Christmas snow drifting all about them; and through it shone the golden windows of coopers selling great yule logs and chandlers selling Christmas candles, and shops of every kind all lit up and decked with evergreens and full of gay and festive things for the hurrying crowds to buy. The windows of St. Mary the Ferry glowed rose and saffron, green and crimson and azure as they rode by, and the sound of singing drifted out to them so faintly that it was as though the carved saints and gargoyles high above them in the spire were singing, instead of real people beyond the glowing windows. The city was still full of a great hurry-scurry that would go on for hours yet, but it was all very silent, and getting more so every moment, because the sounds of hooves and feet and the rumble of cart-wheels were all stilled by the soft white carpet of snow that was being spread in the streets.

Well, so they came riding up their own street at last, and saw the open doorway of the Dolphin House shining through the whirling flakes to welcome them home, and Aunt Deborah standing there with the red glow of the forge fire behind her; and the lovely day was over. They were home again. And presently Piers came back from returning the horses to the inn, and they all sat down to supper in the glow and warmth of the parlour, where Tamsyn's tulip had opened its scarlet petals a little wider since the morning.

Tamsyn was rather sleepy after the long cold ride, and when supper was over and everybody had gathered round the fire—everybody but Piers and Littlest, that is, for Littlest was in bed long ago and Piers had slipped away by himself—she became very sleepy indeed. She sat blinking at the red heart of the blaze, and thinking how the snow would be settling softly, softly, on the decks of the lovely ship and along every ledge and cranny and every carved garland of her high poop and forecastle—a white furred robe for a sleeping Princess—until she had very nearly blinked herself off to sleep. And then quite suddenly she was wide awake again, and thinking that she must go and make sure that her Christmas presents were quite safe. She had hidden them behind a chest in Kit's Castle, but Littlest was so good at finding things he wasn't meant to find, that it would be dreadful if he had discovered her carefully hidden store!

So she got up very quietly, and went away. Nobody asked her where she was going or offered to come with her; nobody ever did ask you where you were going or offer to come with you, round about Christmas, in the Dolphin House; it was a point of honour. She stole upstairs as quiet as a mouse, round and round and up and up until she stepped out into Kit's Castle. It was very cold up there under the snowy roof, and she shivered as she stole across the floor and knelt down beside the chest. The Christmas presents were stored as far behind it as she could reach, and just for one dreadful moment she thought they were not there at all; but she gave a wriggle and managed to reach along a little farther, and there they were, quite safe. She pulled them out a little, and counted them with her fingers. Yes, they were all there; and she got up with a sigh of relief and turned back towards the head of the stairs.

As she passed the door of the cubby-hole which Piers shared with Giles, she saw that it was a crack open, and a bar of yellow friendly light was shining through. (None of the doors that opened from Kit's Castle ever latched properly, unless you were very careful.) Now Tamsyn knew that Piers had not quite finished a little sandal-wood box that he was making for his mother's Christmas present, and she thought he would not mind her looking, because he had shown it to her days ago, and it was so pretty she *did* want to see how it was getting on. So she gave the door a gentle push. People seldom knocked at doors in those days; they just walked in, and if the person inside didn't want them, he simply told them so, or even threw something at them, and they went away again. The door swung inward, and just for an instant she saw Piers without him seeing her. He was sitting at a table in front of the window, with the sandal-wood box in front of him, but he was not working at it. He was crumpled forward across the table, with his head in his arms.

Then the door squeaked, and in an instant Piers sprang up and swung round on her with his head up and his eyes blazing, and demanded in a low, furious voice, 'Can't I have a moment's peace in this house, without somebody poking and prying after me?'

Tamsyn stood quite still in the doorway and gazed at him in horror. She had never seen Piers look like this before, with his face so white and his freckles so black, and his eyes blazing-bright and his beaky nose in the air. He didn't look like Piers at all, but a complete stranger. A dreadful black pit seemed to have opened inside Tamsyn, and all the lovely day fell in ruins because Piers was terribly angry with her and thought that she had been poking and prying after him.

'I'm very sorry,' she said, trying desperately to keep her voice from trembling. 'I—I'll go away.' And she managed quite well, except for a woeful little wobble at the end.

It was a very little wobble, but Piers must have heard it, because suddenly he stopped looking like a stranger, and said gruffly, 'No, don't go away. Come in and shut the door, Tamsy.'

So Tamsyn came in and shut the door, and then she stood with her back to it, still gazing at Piers and gripping her hands together. She said breathlessly, 'I *didn't* come poking and prying! I came up to make sure Littlest hadn't found where I hid my Christmas presents; and I saw your door open, and—and the candle, and I thought you might be finishing the little box; and I hoped perhaps you'd show me how it was gettting on, because it was—was—so pretty, and I w-wanted to see it.'

'Tamsy,' said Piers, 'I'm sorry. I didn't see it was you just for a moment, in the shadow of the door, and I'm sorry I was a beast.' And then he did a rather queer thing: he held out one hand, very slowly, palm upwards, just as though he were trying to gain the confidence of a little frightened wild thing. 'Come and sit on the end of the bed,' he said.

So Tamsyn came and sat on the end of the bed, and smiled at him in a rather watery sort of way because she still felt very odd inside and not at all sure of anything yet. And Piers picked up the little sandal-wood box from among the litter of tools on the table, and began to tinker with the silver clasp, just as though nothing had happened, while Tamsyn watched him and began to feel happier.

'You see, you were quite right,' said Piers after a little while, looking very hard at what he was doing. 'I did come up to finish Mother's box; and then I started thinking about this afternoon instead, and—and wishing things, you know.'

'It's horrid, wishing, and wishing, and not getting what you wish for,' said Tamsyn very softly. 'And she *was* lovely, wasn't she—that ship.'

Piers nodded. And neither of them said any more until he had finished working on the little box and put it away; and then Tamsyn said, 'If you please, *do* you think we could look at the chart, just for a moment?'

So Piers got the chart out of the chest where he kept his clothes, and unrolled it on the table, weighting down the corners to keep it from rolling up again; and he and Tamsyn bent over it in the glow of the rushlight. There were the golden islands washed by sapphire seas, there were the Americas with their snow-capped mountains and broad rivers and forests with jewel-bright birds among the flowering trees, there were the dolphins and the sea-serpents, and the golden sun and the silver moon; above all, there was the ship no larger than a walnut shell, with her sails full of wind and her bowsprit to the New World. Tamsyn gazed at her lovingly, all over, from stem to stern. The three stern-lanterns were the most lovely shape, just like her red tulip; and all at once Tamsyn made up her mind.

'Piers,' she said, 'you know my red tulip?'

'Yes,' said Piers.

Tamsyn slipped off the bed and stood up very straight, and folded her hands in front of her. 'The Wise Woman who gave it to me, she said it would flower at Christmas and bring me my—my heart's desire,' she said. 'I'll give it to you, and then perhaps it will bring you *your* heart's desire instead. And even if it didn't, you'd still have the tulip.' It almost tore her heart in two to think of parting with her red tulip, but she did not regret it for an instant.

Piers looked up from the chart, with his nice half-smile running up into his eyes. 'Tamsy,' he said, 'you *are* a nice person. But you must keep your red tulip; the Wise Woman wouldn't like you to give it away.'

'I—I don't think she'd mind,' said Tamsyn. 'I don't, really.'

'Well, I do,' said Piers, very firmly, but very kindly too. 'You're not going to give me your red tulip, but thank you very, very much for wanting to, Tamsy dear.' Then he began to roll up the chart again. 'Brr! It's cold up here; we'd best be going down to the fire, old lady.'

Tamsyn had not noticed the cold before, she had been too busy thinking about other things, but it certainly was very cold indeed; so cold that the snow that had drifted in under the window-shutters had not melted at all, but lay there, feathery white on the dark sill, sparkling in the light of the tallow dip; and her breath and Piers' breath curled up in little wisps like steam, and her feet were quite numb. So Piers put away his beloved chart and pinched out the tiny crocus flame of the dip, and took Tamsyn's hand in his, and they went downstairs again into the warm bright parlour, to toast their chilblains before the fire until bedtime.

10 *Lullay My Liking*

The snow snowed itself out in the night, and when the sun
rose on the morning of Christmas Eve, all the City was clean and
sparkling in its white furred gown. The streets were unmarked
by any tracks yet awhile, and the sunny sides of the steep roofs were
scattered with sparkling points of light as bright as stars, and every
window flashed in the sunrise, so that once again London was a
City with golden windows.

Aunt Deborah and Meg the Kitchen were very busy all day, with Tamsyn and the Almost-Twins and Bunch and Littlest to help them. After a time Giles and Bunch went to join some boys who were making a slide in the next street, and the others got on better after that, though they still had Littlest to help them.

Work ended early in the Armoury, because of it being Christmas Eve, and after a great deal of handshaking and bobbing and wishing each other a Merry Christmas, the workpeople all went home, and Timothy departed too, with a sprig of bay in his bonnet, whistling down the street on his way to spend Christmas with his own family on the other side of London. Then Uncle Martin arrived back from seeing somebody about something down at one of the wharves beyond Billingsgate, and said that the *Mary Garland* had been sighted coming upriver, homeward bound from the Canaries, he believed, and that pleased Aunt Deborah, because she hoped that now she would be able to buy some fine white sugar. There was generally white sugar to be bought in London after a ship came in from the Canaries.

Uncle Gideon and Uncle Martin hung up the Christmas evergreens between them, while Aunt Deborah stood by and said how clever it was of them, and Tamsyn and Beatrix fetched and carried, and Littlest trotted backwards and forwards, gathering up the bits and pieces.

Giles came home when it was bread-and-raisin time, and afterwards he and Beatrix, Tamsyn and Littlest and Bunch all got themselves up the steep spiral stairway to Kit's Castle, to wrap up their Christmas presents. Littlest wasn't old enough yet to worry much about giving presents, so he sat with his legs stuck straight out before him, in the middle of the floor, with Lammy and his beloved peacock feathers, and did queer complicated things with bits of twine and pasteboard and scraps of wood, while Bunch sat beside him, watching very carefully with his head on one side and his tail giving little interested thumps every now and then. But the other three had each a corner to themselves, and a rushlight to see by, for it was getting dark, and were being very busy and very secret. There was a fourth corner, of course, behind the head of the stairs, which Piers could have had; but he had wrapped his presents up already. They knew that, because Giles had found the parcels when he just happened to be looking in Piers' clothes-chest to see if his own partlet strip had got there by mistake, and now he was clearing up in the workshop.

Tamsyn spread all her presents out and looked at them in the yellow glow of her own particular rushlight, feeling very proud of them. There was a really lovely little orange tree in an earthenware pot, for Aunt Deborah; it had five shiny dark-green leaves on it, and she had been growing it from a pip ever since the spring. There was the partlet strip for Uncle Gideon, which had been kept clean in an old kerchief ever since it was finished; and a wooden horse with green and red stripes round its middle which had cost her a whole penny, for Littlest. There was a cross-stitch crock-holder for Beatrix. (It wasn't so much that she thought Beatrix really wanted a crock-holder, but she couldn't think of anything else, and she couldn't help knowing, although of course she had tried not to, that Beatrix had made one for *her*; so it seemed quite fair.) There was a simply wonderful caterpillar, very big and with tufts of crimson hair along its back, in a little blue pasteboard box with air holes in the lid for it to breathe through, for Giles. Tamsyn had found it in the garden when she was at her wits' end to know what to give him, and it had been a great anxiety to her, because at first it had refused to eat anything except its box; but at last she had tried it on quince leaves, and it liked them and gave up eating its box, so *that* was all right. There was a kerchief for Uncle Martin, and there was another partlet strip—that was for Piers. It was embroidered in scarlet with strawberry flowers and heartsease and maiden pinks, and some of the stitches were rather big because by the time it was finished it was almost Christmas and Tamsyn had been in a great hurry, but it was very pretty, and she did hope that Piers would like it. She had a part share in a kerchief that they were all giving to Meg the Kitchen too, but Beatrix was keeping charge of that.

Mistress Whitcome had given them some soft white paper of a sort they had never seen before, which was really for putting between the folds of the gold and silver tissues in Master Whitcome's silk warehouse; and it was lovely for wrapping up parcels. The Almost-Twins had managed to get most of it, but Tamsyn had some gold paper which had been at the bottom of the pile, and which they had not noticed because it was only gold on one side, and folded with the gold side inmost. Tamsyn had seen the golden glint at one corner, and carried it off while the others were arguing about which of them should have the most tissue paper, so she was quite content. The gold paper was rather stiff—it was the sort that Morris dancers used—and there wasn't very much of it, but she managed to tie a little bit of it round the orange-tree pot, and that left enough for Uncle Gideon's and Piers' presents, and a little bit of tissue-paper for Uncle Martin's and the crock-holder; and anyway, she couldn't have wrapped up the caterpillar or Littlest's horse if she had had all the paper in the world, because the caterpillar would not have been able to breathe, and the horse had the sort of legs that you couldn't wrap up, however hard you tried. When she had finished she sat back on her heels and looked at her parcels, and they really did look nice! White-paper-wrapped and gold-paper-wrapped, and tied up with strands of scarlet silk that had been over from Piers' partlet strip, and the dark, shiny leaves of the orange tree, and the

110

jaunty little horse, and the blue box with the caterpillar in it, all sparkling in the most enchanting and festive way in the light of the tallow dip.

The others had not finished yet, and Tamsyn could hear little rustlings and heavy breathing coming from the other corners of Kit's Castle. It was all shivery-exciting. Tamsyn picked up her treasures and stowed them carefully behind the chest again, ready for the morning. Then she said, 'I'm going to turn round now.' Then she waited while she counted ten, and turned round; but she took care not to look into the other corners even then, because it was a point of honour not to look into other people's corners on Christmas Eve. She blew out her rushlight and went and sat on the play-chest in the window, with her feet drawn up under her for warmth. And next moment she heard Piers shouting from the bottom of the stairs.

'I'm coming up,' shouted Piers, and up he came.

'Don't look!' cried Beatrix, making hurried scuffling noises.. 'Don't you dare look!'

'I wouldn't dream of looking,' said Piers. 'My eyes are tight shut and the key of them is in my wallet.' And he came and sat on the play-chest beside Tamsyn, and they looked out at London together.

The sky was full of stars, sparkling and frostbright, except where the moon rode high above the crowding roofs of the Southwark shore; and the City seemed a city in a fairy-tale, every ledge and cranny deep in sparkling frosted snow, and every carved saint and angel and demon on the tower of every church ermine-hooded and ermine-cloaked. There were lights everywhere, marigold windows in the shadowy walls of houses, and golden lanterns hung before the doors, and every light reflected in the river so that it made two. For in those days people still called Christmas Eve the Feast of Lights, and set candles in every window and lanterns before their doors, to welcome the little King.

'Everything feels as though it was sort of waiting—for something lovely to happen,' whispered Tamsyn. Somehow the snow and the starshine and the lovely expecting feel of Christmas Eve made her not want to talk above a whisper.

'It always feels like that on Christmas Eve,' Piers whispered back. 'Lights, and stars, and snow, and people in their houses, all holding their breath and waiting.'

'How lovely for the sailors in the *Mary Garland* to be home for Christmas,' said Tamsyn. 'Not right to their own houses, I mean, but just—home.' And then she tucked her feet farther under her with a little cosy wriggle, and cuddled closer against Piers. 'At home in Devon at twelve o'clock on Christmas Eve all the animals in the stables kneel down like being in church. Sibbly the Cook told

111

me. I wonder if it's the same everywhere.'

'I expect so,' said Piers.

Tamsyn thought for a little while, gazing out at the starry City. Then she said, 'Tell-true, Uncle Martin's dog, he used to go out and sleep in the stable with Jenny the Mare, on Christmas Eve— not on any other night—just on Christmas Eve. How do you s'pose they know?'

'Perhaps they remember,' said Piers. He thought very hard for a while—Tamsyn could feel him thinking, right down his arm. Then he said, 'I'm sure animals remember all the things that have happened in their families, not just the things that have happened to themselves, as we do. Look how Bunch turns round three times before lying down, because he remembers the time when dogs were wild and made hollows in the long grass to sleep in by turning round and round just like that. Perhaps horses and oxen and donkeys remember what happened in their stable that first Christmas; and dogs of course, there was surely a dog there too. Perhaps they remember so clearly that at midnight on Christmas Eve they seem to see it all again. For just that one moment; lantern light on yellow straw, and their own breath curling up like smoke in the lantern light, and Mary in a cloak cut from the midnight sky, and Joseph in a cloak stained with the warm brown earth, and the little Baby sleeping in their manger, and angels with crimson wings spread round to keep off the cold. And so they kneel down.'

Tamsyn didn't say anything. She was seeing the inside of that stable, the golden light and the kind faces of the cows and horses, and the nice fat little angels with their feathery, crimson wings spread out to keep draughts from the little Baby.

Then the others arrived, because they had finished their wrapping up; and almost at once they heard Aunt Deborah calling up the stairs that supper was ready. 'Coming!' they shouted; 'Coming, Mother,' and 'Coming, Aunt Deborah.' And they went hurry-scurry whirling downstairs, down and down and round and round, like a flurry of falling leaves, with Bunch away in front, and Littlest, who was being allowed to sit up to supper, bringing up the rear.

The parlour was full of candlelight. Candles of honey-beeswax glimmered like stars on every chest and among poor Catherine of Aragon's carved pomegranates on the smoke-hood, and the panes of the windows and every shining leaf of the Christmas garlands reflected back a hundred little, dancing-crocus candle-flames. A great fire of pine logs blazed on the hearth, filling the air with a lovely resiny smell like a fir wood on a hot day; and in the place of honour, in the very middle of the table which was already spread for supper with the best pewter and fine white damask and Aunt Deborah's lovely Venetian goblets, shone the Christmas candle, four times as big as any ordinary candle, making the whole parlour glow and sparkle like a great golden rose. 'A golden rose at Christmas,' thought Tamsyn. 'How nice!' Aunt Deborah was golden too, in her loveliest gown of yellow damask, with pearl drops in her ears and her honey-coloured hair piled high under her black velvet hood, and looking so lovely that Tamsyn thought not even the Queen could look lovelier.

'Look, Tamsy,' said Aunt Deborah. 'Your tulip has come right out, in the warmth of the fire.'

And it had. There it was, in its pot on the sill, a scarlet lamp of a flower, opened wide for the joy of Christmas time.

After Uncle Gideon had said Grace, they all sat down to supper. It was only salt fish and greens and crusty brown bread with whole wheat-grains on top of it, because in those days people ate plain fare on Christmas Eve, while they were waiting for the little King, and feasted royally on Christmas Day, when the waiting was over. But there was a great bowl of frumenty for afterwards, and that was golden too, with the gold of eggs and new wheat and sparkling sugar-candy; and Tamsyn loved it all. She had that shimmery Some-thing-lovely-is-going-to-happen feeling that people do have on Christmas Eve, but she had it more strongly than she had ever had it in all the nine Christmas Eves that she had known before; and the red tulip seemed to feel just the same. It made the salt fish taste simply lovely.

After supper they played Hot-cockles and Cheeses and Hoodman-blind, and Meg came up from her kitchen to help them, and Bunch and Aunt Deborah and Uncle Martin and even Uncle Gideon played too. And when they were all hot and breathless and quite wuzzly in the head from laughing and squealing and running about, Aunt Deborah went to the clavichord, and they all gathered round her for carols. The Dolphin House family always sang carols in Christmas Eve.

Now, in those days foreign Ambassadors and people of that sort always said, when they went back to their own homes again, that England was a nest of singing-birds; and what they meant was this—that in England everybody could sing, not just as people sing in their baths, but as people sing in choirs. It was one of those things you just had to learn, like reading and writing and table manners. Littlest could not sing like that yet, of course, he just made a cheerful noise; but the others could, even Tamsyn; and they all loved singing.

Aunt Deborah touched the ivory keys of the clavichord very gently, as though she loved them, and they gave out a sweet thin music like tiny bells under her fingers; and everybody chose a carol in turn, beginning with Littlest, because he *was* the littlest, and working up through the rest of the family in order of age.

'Littlest first,' said Aunt Deborah.

'Come along, Littlest; what's your choice?' they asked.

Littlest said he wanted the Cockylolly carol.

Everybody looked at each other, and then they looked at Littlest. 'How does it go, Littlest?' they asked.

Littlest stood with his feet planted wide apart, and looked back at them, especially at Tamsyn who was good at knowing what he wanted when the rest of the family did not. 'Littlest wants the Cockylolly carol,' he said firmly. 'Cockylolly on a plate.'

'He wants "King Herod and the Cock",' said Tamsyn.

So they sang "King Herod and the Cock', with Uncle Gideon singing King Herod's bit in his nice deep voice and Littlest puffing out his chest and crowing joyously at the bit where the cock stood up in the dish and crowded and ruffled his feathers.

Then it was Tamsyn's turn, and soon they were all singing:

'Now the holly bears a berry as white as the milk,
And Mary bore Jesus, who was wrapped up in silk:
And Mary bore Jesus Christ, our Saviour for to be,
And the first tree in the greenwood it was the holly,
    holly! holly!
And the first tree in the greenwood, it was the holly.'

So they went on singing, until they came to Piers, and he chose the Cherry Tree Carol; and when that was sung, there was a little silence; and Piers said suddenly, 'I think it would be nice to choose one for Kit. It's his turn now, and it doesn't seem fair that he should be left out of it.'

Aunt Deborah's hands sank into her lap, and she looked round at the family. 'I think it would be nice, too,' she said. 'Who chooses for Kit?'

'You choose for Kit,' said everybody.

So Aunt Deborah thought for a moment, and then she said, 'Let's sing "Lullay my Liking". Kit was very fond of it, and it's time we had a quiet one, anyway.' So they began to sing, very softly this time, and their singing made Tamsyn think once again of the snow and the stars, and the little angels spreading out their warm, feathery, crimson wings to keep draughts off the little Baby; not quite like any of the carols that had gone before. They sang all together at first:

'Lullay my liking, my dear
    son, my sweeting;
Lullay my dear heart, mine
    own dear darling!'

114

Then everyone was quiet, and Aunt Deborah sang on alone, in her high clear voice:

> 'I saw a fair maiden
>   Sitten and sing:
> She lulled a little child,
>   A sweetè lording.'

And then they all joined in again:

> 'Lullay my liking, my dear
>   son, my sweeting;
> Lullay my dear heart, mine
>   own dear darling!'

And suddenly Tamsyn saw pretty Aunt Deborah's face quiver in the candlelight, and she knew that just for the moment Aunt Deborah was not thinking of the Baby in the carol at all, but only of Kit, who had been drowned. And Tamsyn wanted to cry. But Aunt Deborah's face stopped quivering in an instant, and she smiled at Uncle Gideon, and went on alone again.

When the carol was over, Aunt Deborah said, 'Now you, Martin, because you are our guest.'

And Uncle Martin said, "Well, as I am a merchant and often watch for ships, I shall choose "I saw three Ships",' and next instant they were all singing joyously at the top of their voices:

> 'I saw three ships come sailing in,
>   On Christmas Day, on Christmas Day,
> I saw three ships come sailing in,
>   On Christmas Day in the morning.'

While Littlest jigged up and down and hammered Lammy's legs on the back of the clavichord because he liked the tune. They were all making so much noise that it was not until the end of the carol that they heard a loud knocking on the street door, which sounded as though it had been going on for quite a long time.

'Who *can* that be?' said Aunt Deborah, after they had explained to Meg that someone was knocking at the door and she had gone stumping off to see who it was. 'It can't be the Waits, or they would be singing themselves.'

'P'raps it's good St. Nicholas!' squeaked Littlest.

'Silly!' said Beatrix scornfully. 'St. Nicholas never comes until everyone is asleep with their shoes off. He couldn't *fill* their shoes if they were still wearing them.'

Then they heard the street door open, and Meg making the most queer shrill noises of astonishment.

'Who can it *be*?' they said.

Then they heard Meg coming upstairs again in a tremendous hurry, and someone coming up behind her. Next instant she bounced into the stairway arch, and stood there panting and wheezing and looking as though she had had the most tremendous shock, but a good shock, not a bad one, with her face puckered into a huge smile and large tears trickling down her cheeks and bouncing off her chin, sparkling in the candlelight as they trickled.

'Oh, sir!' gasped Meg the Kitchen. 'Oh, Mistress Deborah! — It's Master Kit! Master Kit's come home! He's not drowned at all! He——'

A long arm came round Meg the Kitchen, and hooked her firmly out of the way, and there in her place was a tall young man in ragged clothes much too small for him, who stood blinking in the candlelight and looking round him rather shyly, with his mouth curling up towards his ears in the most entrancing way.

Just for one instant no one moved, not even Bunch. Then the strange young man said, 'I've come home, Mother.' And Aunt Deborah, who had gone very still and white, gave a queer little cry, and sprang up from the clavichord to run to the young man at the stair-head, and Uncle Gideon took one stride in the same direction, and then stopped, so that Aunt Deborah should get there first, which was rather a lovely thing for him to do, when you come to think of it. So Aunt Deborah got there first, and the young man flung his ragged arms round her and hugged her and hugged her and hugged her, as though he was never going to leave off any more, while she clung round his neck and made small joyful crying noises into his ragged shoulder.

Then suddenly everybody was crowding around him, not making very much noise, because when you have been thinking someone drowned for more than two years, and then they suddenly come home, somehow you don't want to make much noise about it, just at first. Tamsyn stood quite still by the clavichord, with her hands clasped before her, and watched. She was not the least bit surprised about Kit coming home and not being drowned after all, because it was just the sort of thing that ought to happen on this night of all the year, and because she had known all along that this was a very extra special Christmas Eve. Only she would have felt just a little lonesome and out of it, if it had not been that Uncle Martin was out of it too, and she thought it would be rather nice if someone remembered her.

Then Piers came and caught her hand and pulled her in with the others, so that she was was not lonesome or out of it any more; and all the noise and rejoicing that hadn't happened before suddenly burst out, and everybody was talking at once, and Bunch was barking all round them, and Uncle Martin joined the throng and Meg the Kitchen burst into tears again, and Aunt Deborah began to laugh and cry at the same time and say over and over again, 'We thought you were drowned, Kit. We thought you were drowned.' And Kit was hugging her against him with one arm and saying, 'I know, dearest, but it's all right now,' and shaking hands with his father with the other hand and saying, 'I couldn't get word to you, sir,' and getting in the most dreadful muddle with trying to do and say two different things at once. And Littlest was standing directly in front of Kit, gazing up at him worshipfully, and repeating over and over again, 'Kit! Kit! *Do* shake hands with Littlest.' And Giles was shouting, 'I say, have you had adventures? I'm sure you must have! I say, I expect you've had tremendous adventures!' And altogether there was so much noise and rejoicing that Tamsyn's head simply went round and round like a top and everything was just a glorious muddle of shimmering light and noise and gladness.

But after a time things quietened down a little, and Kit did shake hands with Littlest, and everything got sorted out after a fashion. Then Aunt Deborah suddenly stopped laughing and crying and became very sensible and motherly, and said Kit must be shrammed and famished, and must have his supper before he said another word (though he had not had a chance to say many words so far). And in an unbelievably short time Kit was sitting down to the table where the Christmas candle was burning brighter than ever, eating up pies and cold ham and marchpanes that had been meant for tomorrow, while everybody crowded round him, and Aunt Deborah sat close beside him and watched him as though she was afraid he would disappear if she let him out of her sight for an instant, and Uncle Gideon, who hadn't said anything much all this time, stood behind the two of them, with his hand on Kit's shoulder.

Between mouthfuls Kit told them how he and two others had been missed in the storm and darkness by the ship that rescued the rest of the survivors of the *Elizabeth* and how they had been picked up next morning by a Portuguese ship bound round the Cape for India; and how of course they had to go on with her for the voyage, working their passages, and so they had had no chance of getting word home to their families that they were safe. He told them about the long voyage to India and back again to Portugal, and how the three of them had hung round the Lisbon docks, living as they could, and hoping for an English ship, until at last the *Mary Garland* had put in homeward bound from the Canaries. And how they had made themselves known to the Captain, and come home with all their troubles behind them, and dropped anchor in the Pool of London scarcely an hour ago, just in time to separate to their own homes for Christmas.

'And never have I seen anything so beautiful as that English ship,' said Kit, helping himself to more raised pie, and breaking off to smile at his mother between mouthfuls. 'Jack Marfield spotted that she was English first—he's got eyes like a hawk—and he let out the most tremendous yell, and then we all saw her, and Tenby said, "We'll be home for Christmas, lads!" and by Cock and Pie! we went clean off our heads for a bit. We nearly didn't get home for Christmas after all—wind dead against us in the Bay—but we just made it—and oh, it's good to be home!'

'There will be three happy homes this Christmas,' said Aunt Deborah, 'if there are no more in all London Town.'

A long, long while afterwards everyone was still gathered in the fire-glow, with no thought of bed. There was so much to talk about on this lovely Christmas Eve when Kit had come back to them. Kit sat on the rush-deep floor, close beside Aunt Deborah's chair, where Aunt Deborah could reach down and touch him every few moments to make quite sure that he was real, and if Aunt Deborah had looked lovely in her golden gown earlier that evening, she was far lovelier now, because her gladness seemed to shine as though a light had sprung up inside her. Tamsyn sat bunched up between Piers and Uncle Gideon's legs in the opposite chimney-corner, and gazed and gazed at the long-lost Kit. He was thin and hard, and brown as a berry and as ragged as the sailor who had brought the letter from Uncle Martin and almost discovered the North-West Passage. He had red hair like all the family—feathery red hair— and long, dancing green eyes, and he looked tremendously nice, but for herself, Tamsyn like Piers best, and so she slipped one hand into his, to show him she did. It was long, long past the children's bedtime, but no one had remembered to tell them to go to bed, and so they had not gone. They sat bolt upright in the fire-glow, with flushed faces and shining eyes, all except Littlest, who was sound asleep long ago, curled up like a puppy beside Bunch among the warm rushes.

Kit had been telling them about India and the riches of the East that he had seen, and about the Portuguese ship, the *Santa Cristobel*, in which he had served, and all the funny and exciting things that had happened during the voyage. And then suddenly he laughed, and reached up over his shoulder to take his mother's hand, and said, 'But I've had enough of the sea. I wanted my one trip, and by Cock and Pie, I've had it!' And he looked across the hearth at Uncle Gideon. 'I've not changed about wanting to be a swordsmith, sir—that is, unless Piers——'

'There's room for you both in the workshop,' said Uncle Gideon.

Then Piers let go Tamsyn's hand and got up and stood looking at Uncle Gideon, with his freckles standing out black across his nose as they always did when he was desperately in earnest; and he said,

'Please, Father, will you let me go from being your prentice? I've not changed, either. I still want to go to sea.'

Then somehow they were all on their feet, and Uncle Gideon said, 'Have you been wanting that, all this time?'

And Piers said, 'Yes, sir.'

'Then why in the name of all the saints in Cornwall, didn't you tell me before?' said Uncle Gideon.

Piers didn't say anything; he just looked at his father in a rather troubled sort of way, because it wasn't the kind of thing you could explain in the middle of a crowd.

And after a moment Uncle Gideon smiled and said, 'Oh, I see. Thank you, Piers. We'll burn your indentures tonight.'

'Thank you, sir,' said Piers, with his freckles blacker than ever, and his eyes shining; and then he turned to Uncle Martin, and asked, 'Uncle Martin, did you mean what you said yesterday—about there being a place for me aboard one of your ships?'

'I did,' said Uncle Martin. 'You shall sail with the *Joyous Venture* in the spring, and here's my hand on it.' So they shook hands with a steady grip and quiver that showed how much they meant it, and Uncle Martin nodded, and said, 'You'll make a good seaman, Piers—one day you'll make a very good seaman.'

'I'll do my best, sir,' said Piers in a sort of joyful croak; and suddenly, for an awful moment, Tamsyn thought that he had forgotten about her share in the *Dolphin and Joyous Venture*, and that he would sail away and find fresh trade routes and discover new lands, and not remember to come back for her at all. But next instant he looked down and caught her eye and gave her a little shared-secret kind of smile; and she knew that he hadn't forgotten, just as certainly as though he had said so; and that one day, when he had risen to be Master of the *Joyous Venture*, he would come back for her. And they would sail out over Bideford Bar and away beyond Lundy into the Golden West, and have adventures together.

Nobody said anything just for a moment, it was as though they were all waiting; and then, suddenly, they heard the Christmas bells!

'It's Midnight!' cried Aunt Deborah. 'It's Christmas Day! Quick, open the windows, my dears, and let Christmas in!'

They tore open windows and set wide the doors; and the starry cold flowed in and the music of the bells. In the golden parlour everybody turned and looked at each other, all except Littlest, who had not woken up. The waiting was over and it was Christmas Day, and the little King had come; and from the towers and spires of London Town the bells rang out the news. From St. Paul's, from the Savoy Chapel, from St. Mary of the Ferry, St. Olaf's and St. Clement Dane and St. Martin in the Fields, from St. Margaret's and the great Abbey, the bells rang out for gladness.

And Tamsyn's tulip on the window-sill, that the Wise Woman had said would flower at Christmas and bring her her heart's desire, stood joyously a-tiptoe, with its scarlet petals held wide, wide open to the stars and the pealing bells.

TITLES IN THIS SERIES